Icarus Falls

Author: Eric Tamburino
ISBN: 9781651893197
Independently Published

Contact:
wheremanandmonstermeet@gmail.com
https://wheremanandmonstermeet.com

Dedication:
To my wife, who supports me in all my endeavors;
in particular, this time-consuming practice we know as writing.

Forward

When I wrote *Where Man and Monster Meet* I didn't fully understand what I was getting myself into. I have always been a storyteller but to be a writer... I'm afraid to say I am still at the very beginning of that journey.

After I launched my first book I fell deep into the world of Indie-authorship. How hard could it be once the book was written? Build a website, give some copies away, post on social media. That is simply not the case.

Without the support of friends and family most authors will be lucky to reach the goal of having 100 copies purchased. I urge you to support your local authors and artists. You can do this by *following, liking,* and *sharing* their content on social media, leaving reviews for their books, and buying their books to give away or just recommending the book to a friend.

With this new book I have realized that writing is not just a hobby of mine, it's a calling. I plan to continue writing, to do my best to bring life to more characters and worlds both to teach and entertain. I have also decided that I will be making much of my work availible for free (at least for a time). This way you can decide the value of the content before you purchase or share it.

I hope you enjoy my first book as well as my second and any others that God is gracious enough to give me time to complete.

Thank you for your support!

Chapter 1

I have to get out of New Hampshire, Autumn thought. She stood in front of her locker, switching out the books she would need for homework, her back to the scuffing of shoes and rustling of other locker doors as the inmates prepared for freedom. Autumn had always thought the high school looked like a prison with its sterile, white linoleum floors and walls, which were only broken up by the firetruck-red lockers.

I have to get out. She couldn't remember when she had first said it, but that phrase kept repeating in her mind as though it were the chorus of her favorite song. She only had to survive three weeks until graduation. Then it would be summer, and after that, college - somewhere far from her parents and the problems of youth. She would finally be on her own.

Her locker door squeaked like the rest of them as Autumn pushed it shut, revealing her two friends Meghan and Ian, who had been waiting.

Meghan stood just barely five feet tall. She wore cut-off jean shorts and a white Hollister t-shirt. Her shoulder-length, jet-black hair hung straight, with bangs pushed off to one side, complementing her oval face. Her perfectly manicured eyebrows accented her large, almond-shaped hazel eyes.

Ian, on the other hand, looked quite comical next to her. Tall and lanky, he towered over both Autumn and Meghan at six feet three inches. His outfit consisted of salmon-colored pants and a light blue shirt with the sleeves half rolled. His light brown hair appeared more tousled than styled, and though neither of them had eyes for each other, Autumn had always found Ian's green eyes to be quite beautiful.

"So... do you have a date for prom?" Meghan asked, a twinkle in her eye.

Meghan had transferred into Manchester Regional High School from an all-girls boarding school at the beginning of sophomore year, and had been a little boy crazy since day one.

"No, I do not," Autumn answered.

"Mike hasn't asked you yet?" Ian pressed.

Mike had been one of Autumn's closest childhood friends. He and his family had moved in down the street when she had been only four years old. The two had grown up together, and as kids, had been virtually inseparable. Then high school had happened. She remembered the first time she had caught him staring at her in class. She hadn't thought anything of it at the time. Then he started bringing her flowers from his mother's shop when he would drop by to see her family. Sure, they hadn't been roses, but she had still been trying to distance herself ever since. Mike was a good friend, but that was all he was. He was a hopeless romantic which Autumn hated, and to top it all off, he had no aspirations of ever leaving his home town.

"Oh Mike has asked," she replied, remembering how she had discovered a rose a day in her locker, each with a corresponding note. After twelve days she had a bouquet of roses and a message that read, *'Would you do me the honor of joining me for prom? Mike'*. Autumn had wanted to vomit. Who spoke like that - *'Do me the honor?'*

"And you said no?" Ian asked, surprised.

"I... "

The door to the adjacent classroom opened and

Derek Mason walked out. He had been kept after class again. His dark, perfectly styled hair seemed to match his black button-down.

Autumn watched as he passed by her and her friends with that ever so subtle strut he seemed to have mastered. Every girl in the school had a crush on him, but Autumn hated everything about him; his friends, the way he did his hair, and how in the winter he wore his father's old leather jacket which was still slightly too big for him. He was immature, impulsive, and always had to have the spotlight. In spite of it all, Autumn desperately wanted him to take her to prom, which was probably why she hated him most.

"Oh, sister, if you're waiting for him, forget it," Ian said, pretending to find something interesting under his fingernails.

"What?" Autumn asked before returning to the conversation. "Ew, no! I said no to Mike because he's just…" she searched her mind for her former answer. "I don't know, romantic and sappy? Does that make sense?"

Ian narrowed his eyes at her, not convinced.

"I don't want to go with Derek!" she stated, looking Ian in the eyes and praying that she wouldn't crack a smile. She had never played poker for a reason.

"So I can take him?" Ian teased.

"Sure, why not!" Autumn declared and pushed by her friends towards the exit. They trailed behind her.

"So have you asked yet?" Meghan questioned.

"No," Autumn replied.

"Has she asked what?" Ian chimed in.

"Has she asked her parents if she can go to Derek's party tomorrow night."

Ian's eyebrows went up. "Yeah, that's going to be a hard no."

Autumn hated the confidence in his answer, but she

knew he was right. The answer would be no. No counteroffers. No sympathy. Just no.

Autumn's parents had become notorious among her friends for being strict. Her mother had been raised Catholic, her father Christian, and although neither of them had been practicing their respective faiths when they had met each other, Autumn's mother had rediscovered her faith somewhere between their wedding and their first child. Autumn's father converted to Catholicism, and now they were two reformed sinners trying to raise little saints.

To make matters worse, Autumn had snuck out to the last party two weeks ago, hoping to spend time with Derek, which hadn't happened. She had been careful to cover her tracks and had all of the proper lies in place, should she need them. Then she had a single beer, and that had been her downfall. On her way home she had gotten pulled over for a dead taillight, resulting in a suspended license. Obviously, her parents had found out. Getting their permission to go to *this* party would be out of the question.

"Well, you'd better figure something out soon, because that's probably the last chance you are going to get to convince Derek to ask you to the prom," Meghan said, giving Autumn a nudge.

Autumn pushed through the double doors and into the heat of the day. Summer hadn't even begun and the temperature had already risen to a balmy ninety degrees. Students stood around in groups, getting in their last conversations of the day before heading home. Mr. Kirkland, the principal, stood at the top of the steps, making sure that students were heading towards their cars.

"I don't know, maybe we should just all go together?" Autumn suggested, knowing Meghan would never concede.

"Absolutely not!" Meghan squealed. "This is a once-in-a-lifetime event, and I will be bringing a date."

"Who are you going with, anyway?" Autumn asked.

"Danny." Meghan said. "Or maybe Carlos."

Autumn shook her head and turned to Ian.

"How about you?"

"Not sure yet. I think a few of the guys from film club are talking about going together. I might tag along with them," Ian answered.

The three friends slowed to a stop. Autumn said good-bye and watched longingly as they headed off to the student parking lot without her. Then she began to walk in the direction of the pickup area, following the beige brick exterior of the building and the large letters that read *Manchester Regional*. She felt like a child all over again. She wished she lived within walking distance.

She walked up to the old 1999 Chrysler mini-van. It was dark green with white patches on the bottom where her father had tried to stop its rusting problem. She pulled the passenger door open.

"Hi, Autumn!" her ten-year-old brother, Joey, exclaimed. He sat in the far back bench seat of the van next to his twin sister Grace, though everyone called her "Gracie". Mikayla, their elder sister of fourteen, sat in the single seat in front of him.

Mikayla didn't look up from her Sudoku book. She loved puzzles and brainteasers, and constantly had a book of vocabulary or math-based games. Autumn didn't mind; the more time she spent with her head in her riddles the less time she pretended to be their mother.

Autumn loved her parents, and though the past year had been a rough one, she understood their rules. She didn't agree with a handful of them, but she understood why they were there. She envisioned herself as an independent thinker. Her own person. Mikayla, on the other hand, seemed to be a half-grown clone of their mother.

"Hi, Joey," Autumn answered as she climbed in and buckled herself.

"How was your day?" Ever since he could talk, he had always asked questions. It had started with the traditional "why" every child asks, but had quickly deepened into much more probing and empathetic questions. Everyone believed he would either be a reporter when he grew up, or a TV host with his own show like Conan or Jimmy Fallon. Gracie, on the other hand, was the polar opposite and rarely talked with anyone outside of the family. When she did talk, it was usually to her brother.

"Same stuff, different day," Autumn answered Joey.

"Mom doesn't like that saying," Mikayla said without looking up from her book.

"I think mom can speak for herself," Autumn retorted.

"Knock it off," her mother said to no one in particular as she looked both ways and pulled out onto the main road. Her mood hung like a storm cloud in the car, and Autumn didn't need to be a detective to know why.

"I'm sorry," Autumn said. "It was one beer."

"We are not discussing this right now," her mother interjected, glancing at the younger children in the rearview mirror. After a minute of silence she added, "What you did was illegal, and now you are paying the penalty. In fact, we all are."

"I thought we weren't talking about it in front of the little angels," Autumn replied.

"Keep it up, you'll lose a lot more than your license."

Autumn subconsciously tightened her grip on her cell phone and bit her lip until it bled.

Chapter 2

Autumn's family lived in a Victorian house, purple with white shutters, which her parents had converted into a bed and breakfast. After many years the interior had been refurbished with modern appliances; but the original wood floors still creaked and the trim still reached halfway up the walls to the floral wallpaper - a constant reminder to Autumn that her grandparents lived in a more up-to-date house than she did.

Located in New England, the bed and breakfast never had much of an offseason. People came in the winter to see the snow and ski the mountains, in the summer to visit the coastline or Boston, and in the fall amateur photographers, "Leaf Peepers", as they were called, came to witness the changing of the leaves.

Autumn's mother ran the bed and breakfast with the help of her children. Autumn's father, on the other hand, had earned a reputation as one of the best auto mechanics in the area, and spent most of his time in a little garage on the edge of their property, trying to build each of his children a college fund.

When Autumn had lost her license, she had upset the balance of her parents' universe. Now her mother had to drive the kids to and from school and her father had to "hold down the fort," losing time to work on vehicles. Less work meant less money, and less money meant the college funds would suffer. Autumn wondered what value college held, other than getting her away from here.

As her mother pulled into the driveway, Autumn watched Father Patrick, the local priest and Autumn's father's best friend from childhood, walk out of the bed and breakfast. The two had grown up together in New Hampshire, and though their lives had gone in very different directions, neither had ever left; a mistake Autumn would be sure not to make.

He smiled and waved as Autumn's mother put the van in park and the sliding door opened to release the children.

In no mood to chat, Autumn stepped out of the van and passed the priest with nothing more than a nod of acknowledgment and headed for the front door.

"I just wanted to say thank you," she heard the priest say to her mother. "I know this was all very last minute, but I think it will do quite nicely."

Autumn stopped with her hand on the front door. She waited, listening.

"Please, we are happy to help. Won't you stay for dinner?" her mother asked.

"You know me, I never pass up a good home cooked meal," Father Patrick answered, before taking out his cell which had begun to ring. He glanced at the caller ID before looking back to Autumn's mother. "But it looks like I have to go. The Bat-signal, you know," he said, referencing his long time favorite superhero.

Autumn shook her head as she opened the door and stepped inside the house.

The bat-signal. He was an idiot.

Upon entering the house, Autumn went directly to her room, needing a minute to herself. She dropped her backpack by the door and laid down on the small but comfortable twin-sized bed, her arms outstretched as if she were preparing to make a snow angel. She glanced over at her bookshelf.

The spine of each book faced her, meticulously arranged in alphabetical order by author. If grabbing one of those books and opening it would have permanently transported her to another world, she would have done it in a heartbeat.

She closed her eyes, breathing in deep and steady, trying to relax before she would have to go back downstairs and help her mom with the everyday chores for the guests.

It was stupid. The bed and breakfast had been her parent's decision and now she had become the slave forced into helping run it.

She longed for college and all its freedoms. To be free of chores and free of rules. She wondered who would help run the place in her absence. Autumn knew her parents couldn't afford to hire help. Then she thought of Mikayla having to pick up the slack, and a wicked smile crossed her face. Then again, Mikayla would probably enjoy it. For all Autumn knew, Mikayla would probably grow up and take the place over just to be like their parents.

At least tomorrow is Friday, Autumn thought. There were no chores on Friday night. But Derek's party was also Friday night and that brought Autumn's mind back to her impending problem. How was she going to get to it?

"Autumn?" her mother called.

"Coming," Autumn answered, rolling off the bed and on to her feet.

She gave a quick look to the mirror on her dresser as she passed by. She stopped for a moment, examining her metallic red hair, her freckled face, and her blue-gray eyes. She adjusted her hair as she left. Cute boys rarely came to the bed and breakfast, but on the rare occasion one did, it always seemed to happen when she looked her worst.

Thursday night chores consisted of general dusting, sweeping, and watering the plants her mother had decorated with. They had six rooms and only four were in use, plus the lobby, the common room, and the dining room.

Autumn weighed her transportation options silently in her mind as she worked.

The party would go late into the night and easily into the morning. On Fridays, her parents wanted the kids in bed around eleven o'clock. Derek lived thirty minutes away so the soonest she would be able to get there would be midnight.

She had asked Meghan if she could drive but Meghan had already lied to her mother about sleeping over at Brittany's. Autumn would have asked Ian, but he had plans to go see a stupid independent movie beforehand.

For a brief moment she thought about texting Mike and asking him to drive her, but that wasn't an option. Sure, he would probably do it. He had a hero complex and he probably already liked her, but they hadn't spoken since she turned him down for the prom. Besides, if he did bring her, then he would be there with her and that defeated the whole purpose.

She could steal her parent's car?

Autumn stopped sweeping for a moment, considering it.

How angry would her parents get? And how much trouble could she get in legally for driving without a license?

She continued to mull it over.

When she finished her chores, Autumn went outside and sat on the front porch with a new book Meghan had lent her. Most of the books in her house were either old beat up classics like Oscar Wilde or Joseph Conrad, which were mainly there for display, or some book that her parents had deemed "good". She had to admit she had enjoyed a few of them like *The Lord of the Rings* but most of the other stuff she hadn't.

Old enough to have her own adult library card, Autumn had hoped to use it more before the incident with her license. She had borrowed Stephen King's *The Shining* and loved it.

She turned over the book Meghan had loaned her,

examining the shirtless man and the wolf howling at the moon in the background, with the red script lettering that read *Love Bites*. Meghan had sworn it to be the new rage.

Autumn shook her head but cracked it open anyway. Only three pages in, she shut the book in disgust and resolved herself to simply sit back and enjoy the rest of the day's sun. It wasn't good literature. In fact, she had found most young adult literature to be oversexualized, oversimplified teen drama and usually not well written. She wanted nothing to do with it. She wanted more Stephen King. She wanted more of *the Greats.*

At six o clock, the sun had sunk low and Autumn made her way to the family's dining room. It had originally been a bedroom before the space had been converted. The actual dining room was reserved for guests of the B&B. Her parents had done this so that no one would disturb the glasses, silverware, or placemats, which Mikayla had to set out every day after school for the following morning's breakfast.

In the center of the family dining room stood a dark, cherry oak dining table and chairs which had been handed down from Autumn's grandparents. A china cabinet stood against one wall, but instead of china, it had been filled with family heirlooms which amounted to virtually nothing as far as money went.

As Autumn walked through the doorway, she noticed something that didn't belong from the corner of her eye and she froze. There, at the end of the table, sat a stranger.

Chapter 3

S he stared at the boy, or rather, young man. He looked a few years older than Autumn. He sat across the table, still as stone except for his eyes, which followed her. His plain, white t-shirt was a stark contrast to his dark features.

"You can't be back here!" she exclaimed, believing that he might be a guest who had simply entered the wrong dining room.

He didn't speak. Instead, he just looked at her as if he had already given his answer and awaited her reply. His eyes moved slowly around the features of her face. It felt as if he were reading her. She had heard that some people could do that, but she had never actually met someone who could.

"You can't be back here," she repeated, a little softer this time but with no less authority.

The double doors that lead to the kitchen swung open and her father stepped through, with serving platter of chicken in one hand and a bowl of mashed potatoes in the other.

"I see you've met our guest," he said to his daughter.

"Yeah. Aren't they supposed to be on the other side of that door?" she motioned to the separator.

"I'm sorry, sweetie, I meant he is staying with the family. He is not a visitor."

Autumn looked back at the young man and saw that his eyes hadn't changed. They were dark, like two black holes that seemed to soak everything in. He sat quietly observing their interaction, the way some people will watch the chimps at the zoo.

Who is this creep? She thought.

The divider door swung open and the rest of the children filed in just as Autumn's mother came from the kitchen carrying the rest of dinner; a bowl of mixed vegetables and a salad. Autumn watched Mikayla's face as she noticed the stranger at the table.

Joey settled into his usual chair and met the stranger's gaze. They were roughly two feet apart and looked as if they were having a friendly staring contest. Joey broke the silence.

"Hi!" he said.

"Hi," the young man answered.

Autumn didn't know why, but she thought maybe he would have a really rich dreamy voice to go with his dark features. Granted, she had initially thought him a creep, so maybe she had expected it to be more thin and raspy. Either way, his voice was bland and average, which surprised her.

"I'm Joey," the boy continued. "What's your name?"

"Icarus," the young man said with a smile.

"How about we hold the introductions until after grace?" Her father asked, looking at Joey. Joey nodded. The rest of the family made their way to their seats. Her father took his seat at the head, his wife across from him. Mikayla and Autumn sat at his left, Joey and Grace on his right. Icarus sat between their father and Joey.

They said the blessing and began their meal.

"Kids, there is someone I would like you to meet," their dad said, as he began passing the food around. "This is Icarus."

"That's a funny name," Joey stated before his mother shot him a look. Though Joey had a gift for conversation, he still needed work on his tact.

"Icarus... isn't there an old story about him?" Mikayla asked.

"There is," the stranger answered. "He and his father were trapped on an island by an evil king and so Icarus's father gathers some bird feathers and makes wings for them to fly away with. When they are up in the air, Icarus is so excited he flies higher and higher. His father had warned him before they had left not to do that because the sun would melt the glue in the wings. But Icarus didn't listen, and his wings fell apart."

"What happened next?" Joey asked.

"He fell into the ocean and died."

"So you're named after a dead guy?" Mikayla asked.

"Aren't we all?" Icarus answered before adding, "My father is a history teacher. He thought it would be funny as my last name is Falls."

"Your name is Icarus Falls?" Autumn asked in disbelief. "I thought I had it bad."

"Why?" Icarus asked. "What's your name?"

"Autumn," she said.

"What's wrong with that?" Icarus asked.

"The leaves turn red in the fall and my hair is red."

"I see," Icarus commented looking around the table.

Autumn's mother and sisters were both blonde, and her father and brother both had brown hair.

"Where does it come from?"

"Her grandmother," Autumn's father answered. "On my side."

"I'm Mikayla," Mikayla introduced herself, "and that is Grace, but we all call her 'Gracie'. She doesn't talk much."

Grace waved down the table.

"And you must be Mrs. Williams," Icarus concluded. "Very nice to meet you all."

"Father Patrick asked if Icarus could stay with us a little while, while I fix his car," Mr. Williams said.

Oh great! Just what we need; strange men living in our house, Autumn thought. But then again they almost always had strange men and women in their house, thanks to her parents' business. *Whatever.* She had bigger problems to deal with.

"And he will be driving you to school each morning and picking you up with the van," her mother added.

Autumn's heart fell.

The stranger with the weird name was going to drive them to and from school in the minivan every day, for however long it took her father to fix his car. Autumn wanted to die. From which circle of hell had this nightmare been dredged up? She opened her mouth to protest but then thought better of it. She had three weeks until the end of high school. Best not to rock the boat.

Supper dragged on after that. Mrs. Williams asked each kid about their day, and Icarus seemed to pretend he somehow had been a part of the family since the beginning, listening and acting interested. Autumn could feel her phone burning a hole in her pocket as the seconds slipped by. She had to text her friends.

After the meal the kids all marched their dishes and silverware into the kitchen, and after rinsing them off, placed them in the dishwasher.

When Autumn finally got to her room, she whipped out her phone and began to text out a message. After a few moments, she decided it was too much to text. She would explain it to them tomorrow. She tossed the phone on her bed. Autumn thought about doing her homework, but she had finished all of it in study hall except math, her last class of the day, so she would do it tomorrow. She took the book out of her pack and left it opened on her desk to a random page, just in case her parents dropped in. Then she opened the drawer and slid out her notebook. It was not a school notebook or a diary. Autumn thought diaries were just as silly as the word itself. They were childish in her eyes. This notebook meant much more to her. It was her writing notebook. In another year, when she was away at school, she would take after all the greats and pour herself a glass of gin, or maybe vodka, and she would pour out her soul along with it. Her eyes scanned each page. They contained mainly short stories, broken up by ideas for her novel that she would write someday. As she turned to the next blank page, she put her pen to paper and began to write about something far away from New Hampshire.

Chapter 4

A utumn awoke to the beeping of her alarm, and after running through the shower and getting dressed, entered the kitchen and her mother's chaos.

Her father woke up long before any of the children and they only ever saw him in the evenings and on Sundays. Mikayla would oversleep and then take too long in the shower.

Gracie and Joey were sitting at the table quietly waiting for breakfast, while her mother tried to organize guest orders and arrange plates of food correctly. Her mother could keep everything straight for the guests, but when it came to her own children, she left a lot to be desired. Every day began like this, and it drove Autumn to the brink of her sanity.

The door opened and Icarus walked in. For a moment, Autumn had forgotten. Then he turned and caught her eye and she remembered. *The creepy staring guy who lives with us now.* He glanced over at the two kids sitting at the table waiting for their breakfast, and then over to their mother as she cycled through pages of her tiny notepad.

"Can I help with anything?" he offered.

"What?" her mother asked, startled. "No. Actually, yes! It was scrambled eggs with the bacon. Right?"

Icarus raised an eyebrow.

"Sorry, just thinking out loud," she continued. "Did you ask me something?"

She transferred the bacon from the plate with the fried

eggs to the plate with the scrambled eggs and added a helping of hash browns to each.

"Hold on a second," she said, picking up all four plates like a professional server and heading towards the door. She looked at the children as she passed by. "I'm sorry, I'll be right back. Autumn, can you get these two breakfast before they have to leave?" She backed through the door and disappeared.

Autumn looked at Icarus and smirked.

"Yeah, it's always like this, if that's what you're wondering," she said. "Top shelf on the left. Can you get the honey nut cheerios for Gracie?" she asked, pointing.

Icarus walked over to the cabinet and grabbed them. Autumn handed him a bowl and a spoon. "The milk's on the door in the fridge."

She turned to Joey.

"Scrambled eggs and toast?"

Joey smiled.

"How about you?" she asked turning back to Icarus.

"I'm fine, thanks. Not really a breakfast person."

Autumn shook her head and began cracking eggs. *Not a breakfast person. Right.*

Icarus brought the cereal and milk over to Gracie, and she thanked him.

Autumn cooked up four eggs scrambled and four pieces of toast, each with a generous helping of butter. She split it between two plates and gave one to Joey before sitting down at the table with her own.

Mikayla entered the kitchen just as they all finished eating.

"What's for breakfast?" she asked.

Autumn handed her a banana as she walked by.

"Everyone be in the van in five minutes," Autumn said as she went back to her room to grab her bag.

When Autumn got out to the van, she was surprised to find all of her siblings buckled and waiting. They were on time for once. Autumn rode in the passenger seat and directed Icarus to the middle school. The kids made it in before the ring of the first bell.

Then it was just the two of them, alone in the car.

Autumn reached over and turned on the radio, twisting the dial until a pop station came on. Her mother only ever played the car radio around Christmas to hear the carols. The rest of the year, she told the children that their conversations would be more stimulating than music. Autumn doubted her mother had told Icarus.

"What type of music do you like?" Icarus asked.

"Everything," Autumn answered.

Icarus shook his head and smiled.

"What?" asked Autumn.

"Everyone says that."

"Well, it's true."

"You like country?"

"Yes."

"Opera?"

"No."

"Screamo?"

"Ok fine, I like most music; *normal* music. Classic rock, pop, alternative." Autumn answered, irritated.

The ten-minute drive from the middle school to the high school usually passed in a flash, but today it may as well have been a journey walking across a desert barefoot. Icarus pulled up to the curb and let Autumn out. She grabbed her bags and shut the door without so much as a thank you. He watched her.

What does he expect? A kiss? Or a wave? She shook her head as she turned to her friends, who were waiting for her at the bottom of the large granite steps.

"Who is *that*?" Meghan asked, pointing to the minivan.

"Icarus," Autumn answered, without even turning.

"He's hot," Meghan stated.

"Icarus?" Ian asked.

"Yeah, weird name, I know. He needs some work done on his car, so he's paying my dad back by being our chauffeur."

"Invite him to the party!" Meghan exclaimed.

"Absolutely not!"

"But he can drive you! Don't you see? It's fate! The universe sent you a wicked hot guy to drive you to the party, so you can have a different hot guy ask you to prom, and I can take the wicked hot guy off your hands."

"She has a point," Ian joined in, holding the entryway door open for both girls as they entered the school.

Autumn considered it for a moment. *No.* She couldn't bring Icarus.

"I'll think about it," she lied.

"Well you'd better think fast," Ian said. "You only have a few hours once school gets out."

Autumn grimaced.

Chapter 5

Autumn didn't believe in watching the clock, but today she couldn't help it. She had a lot to figure out and very limited time to do it, and classes were frankly an impediment to her ability to do that. Pretending to pay attention took just as much energy as actually doing it. Luckily, most of the teachers had no desire to start anything new. Even they didn't want to be there. To top it all off, she now had the added effort of avoiding Mike.

She made it through most of the day without bumping into him. She had first period English, second period French, third period study hall, lunch, etc. Then it was finally over. She went to her locker and switched out the books she would need for the weekend.

She had almost escaped when Mike finally caught up to her.

Just as Autumn, Meghan, and Ian pushed through the front doors, she saw Mike waiting at the bottom of the large stone steps, like a puppy waiting for its master.

"Autumn!" He called.

"Oh crap," she whispered.

"Hey, can I talk to you for a sec?"

He climbed the eight steps two at a time.

"Look, Mike, I don't want to-"

"I'm sorry."

Autumn stopped.

He was sorry? For what? Embarrassing her? Embarrassing himself? For being so hopelessly stupidly romantic? She looked to her friends as they continued on to the bottom of the stairs. Ian made a face, as if to say good luck.

"I'm sorry if I made you feel uncomfortable," Mike continued.

You think? Autumn wanted to scream. He *had* made her uncomfortable, and ironically here he was apologizing for it and doing it all over again.

"It's just that..."

Autumn looked for a way out, an excuse to leave before he could finish his sentence, but no opportunities or magic portals appeared. She knew what he was going to say. She had known it for a long time. But if he never said it out loud, if she never heard him say it, then maybe, just maybe they could pretend it wasn't the case.

"I like you," he said.

Autumn's heart skipped a beat. Not out of love, the way she had read about in books, but out of sheer panic. She could feel her face getting hotter and hotter, and she knew if she didn't get out of there soon her face would match the color of her hair. At least he hadn't said he loved her. That would have been a whole different nightmare.

"Yeah, that's usually what a bouquet of roses means," she said, trying to dismiss him.

"No, I like, really like you," he continued, reaching for her hand. "I have for a long time and-"

Oh no. She looked around hoping that none of the nearby students were listening. Students were still pouring out the door behind her and walking by on the steps.

"I get it if you don't want to go to prom with me. I just needed you to know."

Autumn looked longingly to her friends, then to the

24

minivan, then down to her hand which Mike had taken in his. She pulled it away. *Oh Mike, you idiot. Someday you will make someone really happy, and she will probably be just as sweet an idiot as you.* She *needed* this to end. *Why can't we just be normal friends?*

"I'll think about it," she muttered, trying to let him off easy. "I have to go."

Autumn pushed past him, dropping her eyes to the ground. She walked straight for the minivan at a pace just short of jogging. She avoided the gaze of her friends and everybody else who might be looking. She wanted to kill someone, she wanted to cry. Why had he had to tell her in the middle of the steps in front of the entire school?

She pulled open the van door to an ambush of questions from Mikayla.

"Did he just ask you to prom? Does mom know? Are you two in love? Did you-"

"Shut up!" She barked, knowing that she would probably be grounded for yelling at her younger sister. She didn't care. She needed to be anywhere but here.

She turned to Icarus without buckling in.

"Drive."

Chapter 6

The heat hung in Autumn's room, making her feel as if she were cooking in an oven. She watched as the drops of condensation on the glass of water on her nightstand trickled down the glass into a tiny pool. She sat with her ear to the door, sweating from the heat, or maybe just all of her nerves as she listened. She had picked out her outfit for the party, and hidden it under her bed while she went through all of her Friday night routine.

Though she hadn't had chores, she had spent most of the time she would have preferred to be writing in her notebook explaining the situation with Mike to her mother. Not by choice, but because the first words out of Mikayla's mouth when they got home were to tattle to her mother about Autumn telling her to shut up. Surprisingly, her mother hadn't punished her. She simply told her to do something nice for Mikayla and not to let it happen again.

Autumn had been roped into helping with dinner. Then, after they ate, Autumn had stayed to watch the Friday night movie with the family before finally getting into her pajamas and brushing her teeth.

Now she waited, ear to the door, to be sure that everyone had gone to sleep. It had been almost an hour, and she felt pretty confident that no one remained awake. *One of the few good things about early bedtime rules.* She heard a few sounds, but they all sounded like the familiar noises the house made on the nights she couldn't sleep. Deciding she had waited long enough, Autumn moved silently across her room and changed into the outfit she had picked; a sundress, blue, with lilies on it. She applied a base layer of foundation and added mascara. She finished off her preparation with a nice shade of her mother's lipstick she had "borrowed". Then, still having no plan as to how she would get to the party, she grabbed her purse and headed to the door. She waited a moment, listening again; then she stepped out into the hallway. She crept down the hall, careful to avoid all of the noise spots she knew about.

When she got to the top of the steps, she could see light coming down the hallway. She froze, wondering if her parents were still awake. *Probably not.* Sometimes they left the light above the kitchen sink on. She listened for a minute. No conversation, no clinking of dishes, nothing. She had made it halfway down the stairs when it hit her that it could be Mikayla getting a glass of water. If it was, Mikayla would rat Autumn out.

Autumn moved off of the stairs and towards the door with the grace of a ninja. She turned the corner and looked down the hallway towards the light. She moved closer, slowly, careful not to make any noise. She peeked in through the doorway. There, at the counter, sat Icarus.

She should have figured. The kinda cute, or rather "wicked hot", creepy kid that now lived with them.

He had his head down. Autumn watched, wondering if he had somehow fallen asleep, sitting up with his head in his hands. Then she heard the sound of a pen furiously scribbling. He was writing. Maybe fate wanted her to take Icarus with her - or maybe she had just better turn and leave. She pivoted and heard the floorboard creak beneath her. She held her breath. She looked back at Icarus. *Screw fate*, she thought. Icarus looked up and Autumn quickly raised her finger to her lips gesturing for him to be silent. He nodded. She motioned towards the back door behind him. He stood up, shut his notebook, and went outside, taking the book with him. Autumn watched in horror, waiting to hear something, but he made no sound. He walked as silently as death. Even when he opened the door he somehow remained noiseless. She followed him outside and eased the door shut behind them.

"Do you have the keys?" she asked in a whisper.

Icarus reached into his pocket and produced the keys to the minivan, which he had apparently forgotten to leave in the key basket.

Autumn took a deep breath. *Moment of truth.*

"Wanna go to a party?" she asked.

Chapter 7

The night began to cool off, leaving the air thick and humid. Autumn watched the headlights of the car cutting through the fog. Her hair tossed gently as they rode with the windows down. Icarus drove calmly, not as cautious as her mother, but not as idiotic as the few other young men she had ridden with. He seemed to have the respect for the vehicle that only comes with experience.

Autumn took a deep breath of the fresh air and slowly released it. Her heart was racing and though her mind still had many questions there was a sense of relief that she had taken a chance on Icarus and it was paying off.

"What were you doing up? You're not a vampire, are you?" she teased.

A smile crossed his face.

"No. I'm not a vampire. Good thing too. Your family invited me in."

Autumn thought back to when she had read Bram Stroker's *Dracula*. Vampires had to be invited in by the host; one of the many rules forgotten by modern portrayals.

"You sure seem to know a lot about them," Autumn said jokingly, though she couldn't help glancing at the rosary her mother left hanging on the rearview mirror.

Icarus laughed.

"So what were you doing?" she repeated.

"Writing. It helps me gather my thoughts sometimes

when I can't sleep."

Autumn could relate. There had been many nights when after tossing and turning, she had laid awake under the covers with her penlight and her notebook, trying to make sense of the world.

"What is it about?" she asked.

"It?"

"Your book," she said, before realizing it might not be a book. "Or is it a diary?

Icarus thought for a moment.

"I suppose you could call it a diary of sorts. It's more of a collection of letters. I've always found it stupid to write 'dear diary,' so I address each new entry to someone I have known personally and write whatever it is I need to say to them."

Autumn liked the idea. She had always said she didn't keep a diary, but rather a journal, for a similar reason. It was a strange idea, but clever. It suited him.

"So why is it so important for you to go to this party anyway?" Icarus asked.

Autumn considered his question. She didn't want to tell him about Derek. For that matter, she didn't want to tell anyone she was going for Derek, but she had already trusted Icarus to sneak her off to this party; why not trust him with her stupid secret?

"There's a guy," she began.

"Oh?"

"No," she said, quickly realizing it sounded as though she were sneaking out to see a secret boyfriend. "There's this guy at school. He's super popular and all the girls like him."

"So, you also like him?" Icarus asked, after a moment of silence.

"Ew. No!" Autumn exclaimed. "I don't know... I think he's kinda cute."

She said it more to the night air out the window than to Icarus.

"Anyway, this party is the last major opportunity I have to get him to want to take me to prom."

She cringed as she said it out loud. It sounded desperate.

"I don't know, I always thought prom was kinda stupid," Icarus said.

Autumn's anger flared. She had confided in him and this was how he chose to use the information? To make fun of her?

"Sounds like someone didn't get laid at his prom," she said, coldly.

He glared at her. It was the first time he had taken his eyes off the road, and for a minute Autumn didn't believe that he wasn't a vampire. She had forgotten how dark his eyes were, and now they seemed somehow darker. There was a menacing nature in them that sent a chill through her. In spite of their darkness, Autumn couldn't help but notice the expression they held. There was so much to read in those eyes.

He shifted his gaze back to the road.

"I didn't mean to offend you," he said. "I said I thought *prom* was stupid, not you."

"It's fine," she replied, crossing her arms over her chest. "I think it is too."

Chapter 8

Icarus pulled the mini-van up half over the curb and half onto the lawn, at the back of a long line of cars which had done the same. Derek lived in a new neighborhood development. Autumn scoffed as she looked at the large, white colonial house with green shutters.

"So this is how the rich live," she mumbled, as Icarus rolled up the windows and they exited the vehicle. They walked up the front lawn, the faint throbbing of a bass drum reverberating through the otherwise still night.

"So what do you want me to do?" Icarus asked.

"About what?"

"About this guy you like?"

Autumn laughed. She wondered what he thought he could do. She imagined him walking up to Derek in his Icarus Falls fashion, shaking Derek's hand, and saying, "Hi, have you ever considered asking Autumn to prom?" She sucked in a deep breath of air and held it in for a moment. *It's bad enough you're here at all,* she thought.

"You can find a corner of the wall to hug, not near me, and blend in," she replied.

Icarus nodded.

The door opened to the deafening music which violated the quiet stillness of the summer night. They inched into the packed house and the door closed behind them.

Autumn stood stunned by it all. The party at Meghan's

house had been a few friends and a few popular kids but this... this was chaos. She didn't recognize most of the people in front of her. Had Derek invited the whole school?

She turned to Icarus, hoping he had not seen how clueless she had been, but he was gone.

"Great," she muttered as she pushed into the crowd, hoping to find Meghan and Ian.

She had fallen into the ocean in the middle of a hurricane, and she fought against the overwhelming chaos as she moved through the entryway towards the living room. Two hands clasped her over the eyes, and she heard a voice shouting into her ear, "Guess who!"

Autumn didn't bother trying to reply. She brushed the hands away and felt a wave of relief as she turned to see Meghan.

"Where's Ian?" she asked.

Meghan shook her head that she couldn't hear.

Autumn made a gesture indicating someone a head taller than them.

Meghan laughed and pointed to the center of the living room. A small crowd had begun dancing and Ian was in the center, already hammered by the looks of it.

Meghan took her by the hand and led her to a less populated corner of the room.

"Hey, girl! You made it! Oh my gosh, you are never going to believe-" Meghan stopped and looked Autumn up and down. "You look like a church girl."

"And you look like a slut, ok?" Autumn answered, starting to feel insecure about her choice of sundress.

Meghan laughed. "Let's get you a drink!"

"I don't know-" Autumn began to answer, but Meghan dragged her over to a table with a giant punch bowl on it. Meghan grabbed a new solo cup, dunked it into the pinkish-red liquid, and handed it to her friend before dunking her own in.

"Have you seen Derek?" Autumn asked.

"He's around."

Autumn's eyes began to scan the crowd as she put the plastic cup to her lips, her eyes peeking over the rim.

"You're not ready yet," Meghan laughed, tipping Autumn's cup up a little higher.

Autumn drank it in. She knew she needed a buzz if she was going to talk to Derek. *Ok, not that I need it,* she thought. *But it would certainly make it easier.*

The music boomed on, and she watched all of the people swaying back and forth as if they were all in a trance. Part of her wanted to be like that. To just tap into the energy and completely lose herself in the moment. But there was another side of her where she felt she would never understand. She took another sip from her solo cup.

"So, what's the plan?" Meghan asked.

Autumn looked around. She wasn't an introvert, but she wasn't a party goer either. She loved her friends and she loved her books. Anxiety began to flood her mind at the sensory overload of the cacophony and sheer madness around her. *Get it together,* she thought. People glanced at her casually, probably wondering what she was doing there to begin with. She hadn't been at any of the other parties. Then again they probably hadn't been either. Or maybe they were thinking that she looked silly in her sundress with a red solo cup and a face that said 'I have no idea what I'm doing here.'

"Waiting for the right opportunity," Autumn said.

Meghan laughed. "You have to create your own opportunity! Like me."

Meghan had no problem talking to boys, a skill Autumn envied. But Autumn knew that didn't mean Meghan had it all together. Most of the time Meghan came off as too interested, or even "easy," which drove away a lot of the boys she actually liked and attracted another breed which she tended to have short term relationships with.

"Loosen up, girl!" Meghan said, reading the thoughts on Autumn's face. "Come on, let's dance!"

Meghan grabbed her hand, and half led half-dragged Autumn onto the makeshift dance floor, before Autumn could come up with an excuse. Then they were in the throes of it all. Meghan immediately got into it. She had sworn to Autumn that she had never taken dance lessons, but Autumn found that hard to believe. Meghan moved with the grace of a ballerina, and the confidence of a stripper. Autumn, on the other hand, did not. She stood stiff as a board while other people bumped, bounced, and gyrated around her, occasionally offering the friendly nod or thumbs up that said: "it's all good here." Unfortunately, she knew that would not last forever; she had to get into it or get out of it.

She took another sip of her drink and closed her eyes, listening to the music. Starting simple, she began to sway her hips to the rhythm. The alcohol began to sweep over her like a warm fuzzy blanket. The weight of the world had seemed to lift for a little while. She kept her eyes closed, trying to feel the music and not the potential judgment. She dipped her head down, then ran her fingers through her hair as she came up, tussling it, and hoping she looked just as seductive as some of the girls she had seen in music videos. She opened her eyes to see Meghan laughing; the good type of laughter, not the judging type. Autumn giggled and they continued to dance.

Autumn had not been to many parties, and the few she had been to hadn't been like this. She had been at smaller ones, "get-togethers," and she had often found herself feeling more like an alien watching a group of teenagers, studying them in their habitat and wondering what it must be like, rather than being one of them. But this time she began to understand. The music, the dancing, the chaos – it was liberating. For the first time since the beginning of senior year, she started to feel like a kid again. Her problems melted away. She glanced over at Ian, and saw him in the middle of a dance circle. Everyone loved him. *This is it. This is what it is all about.* She knew, no matter what happened in the days to come, she would remember this night forever. Then she saw Derek ten feet away and she froze. She couldn't see his dance partner.

She knew she could do it. She could talk to him. Autumn debated having another drink first. *No.* She was going to push through those ten feet of people, and she was going to dance with him. She imagined him holding her close. But the thought of school on Monday morning, without all of the liquid courage, interrupted.

She had almost taken that first step towards Derek, when Meghan grabbed her by the shoulder and turned her in the opposite direction.

Lexi had come over. One of Meghan's gossip buddies.

Meghan shouted something that Autumn could barely hear. She did, however, catch the name "Icarus".

Oh no, she thought.

Lexi motioned for them to follow her and led them to the back of the dancefloor. Several people stood up against the countertop bar and Eric, from Autumn's chemistry class, seemed to be pretending he knew something about bartending, slinging cheap beers to his patrons. It wasn't until she got to the entryway and looked into the kitchen that Autumn realized why she had been called away.

Chapter 9

There he was – Icarus Falls - sitting on the countertop with three of the most popular girls in school all gathered around him, vying for his attention. Autumn wasn't close enough to hear the story he told as he waved his beer casually back and forth through the air. He looked like he belonged; his posture, his confidence, even the way he held his beer. He looked comfortable; he looked as though he were at home.

His eyes caught hers.

"Ah, here she is now!" Icarus called, and motioned to her.

Autumn thought about pretending she hadn't heard him, but she knew it was too late. Besides, he had waved. She knocked back the rest of her drink, and cursed too quietly for anyone to hear as she walked over to where he sat on the counter.

"This girl," Icarus said, "is the sun and the moon."

Concerned about her reputation and ending this situation, Autumn didn't care about his grossly poetic line.

He reached out, took her hand, and with a quick gesture spun her in close to him as if they had been dancing.

Taken aback, Autumn almost spun around to face him and knock him off of the counter, but then she heard his voice behind her ear, just loud enough for her to hear beneath all the noise as he leaned in close to her.

"If you want that boy's attention, trust me."

She stood in front of him now, his arms draped around her, and his face buried in her hair.

She looked at the girls as she now stood in the center of them. In spite of all of their falsities, they could not hide their disbelief.

"How did you meet your boyfriend?" Icarus asked the girl to his right, his face finally out of Autumn's hair.

Autumn didn't hear Gina's response though. Her focus had shifted to Emily, the informer of the school, the leech of the popular crowd and a busy body before her time. Emily had slipped away and Autumn watched as she made her way through the crowd. She watched carefully as that snake of a girl slithered through their classmates, and what she had feared began to play out in front of her. Emily tapped Derek on the shoulder.

Oh no, she thought. She had to get away from Icarus. Derek wasn't going to understand what she was doing; *she* didn't even know what she was doing. She tried to step forward, but Icarus's arms tightened around her. Derek turned. He looked right at them. Frustrated, she pried the can of cheap beer from Icarus's fingers and began to chug it until nothing remained. Then she tried again to separate herself from Icarus and, this time, he let her go.

Her mind raced for ways to salvage the situation. She would need a logical explanation for Derek.

Icarus's voice cut through the party.

Autumn turned back. Shannon had already taken the spot where Autumn had been and had draped his arm around herself.

"Hey, babe! I'm out!" he called to Autumn, pointing to his beer can. "Grab me another?"

Anger swelled, along with a flood of tears, and Autumn bit her lip. *Screw you,* she thought. *Screw you and everyone at this party.* She felt stupid for coming in the first place. She was a wallflower. Her idea of a party was having a few friends over, drinking soda, and staying up past eleven to watch a chick flick. *Did you think you were just going to walk up and talk to Derek? Or that he was going to just walk up to you?*

She turned as the first tear slipped down her cheek. Maybe he didn't see, she thought, but she knew Derek had seen it all. She dropped her head and began to move directly towards the front door. Then she remembered that she couldn't drive, and even if she ignored the fact that her license had been suspended, Icarus had the keys.

Screw him. Screw you, Icarus Falls.

Blending right into her family and her life like a chameleon, he had even started to win Autumn over a little but now she saw his true colors. She had been wrong about him. She didn't know him at all. She had come to this party with a complete stranger.

With only one course of action left, she headed back to the punch table and plunged a solo cup into the punch bowl. She began to see visions of her filling up two cups and dumping them all over Icarus and that tramp, Shannon. Then another where she got a fresh beer can and threw it at him. *Or maybe shake it so it explodes.* She wondered if that worked with beer cans the way it did with soda. She knocked back the glass of punch, and then dipped it in again. This one would be for Icarus Falls.

"Your boyfriend seems like a tool," a voice said from behind her.

"He's not my boyfriend," she answered, doing her best not to burst into tears.

She looked for another cup, but didn't find one. One glass of punch over the head would have to be enough. She turned, and saw Derek behind her.

Her heart skipped.

"Derek, hi," she said, hoping her face hadn't revealed

how awkward she felt.

"Are you ok?" Derek asked.

"Yes thank-" she completed the thought with a belch.

Mortified, Autumn could feel her face turning red but Derek didn't seem to notice.

"So who is that guy, anyway? What's he doing at my party?"

"He's-" she thought about lying but couldn't think of anything good, "my driver."

"Your driver?" Derek asked in disbelief.

"Yeah. I got my license suspended a little bit ago."

"I heard about that. Over one beer, right? That's just stupid," Derek said, finishing his drink.

Autumn laughed nervously, "Yeah."

Derek dipped his cup lightly into the bowl of punch.

"Come dance with me," he said.

He led her by the hand and she followed him to the center of the dance floor. Everything seemed to fade away. The people around her were just blurs swaying. They spun gently and slowly like leaves in the fall until the whole world began to spin. Then hot breath on her lips, then her neck. Derek kissed her. He kept kissing her. It had to be a dream, a perfect dream. She floated through the crowd, light as a feather. She watched the lights from his arms. She saw stairs. Then everything went black.

Chapter 10

A utumn awoke in her bed, her stomach racked with pain. She needed food, but couldn't fathom the idea of actually eating anything. She tried to sit up but a white-hot pain flashed through her mind as she moved her head. She wanted to cry it hurt so bad. *What's wrong with me,* she thought. Her parched lips tasted like vomit and the faint smell of nail polish remover made her nauseous. She licked her dried out lips again, trying desperately to moisten them. In her half-awake state, she had the surreal feeling of each drop of sweat forcing its way through her skin. Her body burned in spite of the moisture. Her bedsheets were soaked and the air felt heavy. Her sweat turned cold and vomit began to force its way up into her throat. She hurriedly rolled to the edge of her bed where her trashcan stood, and gracelessly tumbled over the edge onto the floor.

What's going on? she thought, as her body continued to fail her. Her mouth opened as her throat constricted, and her stomach convulsed involuntarily. Nothing came up. She choked for air, laying on the floor unable to move.

"Keep quiet. You don't want to wake your parents," she heard Icarus say, and an arm slipped around her, helping her up. She tried to nod, but her head rolled lazily to the side. Together they hobbled across the hall from Autumn's room to the bathroom. Icarus gracefully draped her over the edge of the bathtub and turned on the cold water. Then he shut the door and locked it.

"Oh God," Autumn whispered. "If you end this... I promise..."

Icarus placed her hands under the cold water, and after dousing a washcloth, began to dab her face and the nape of her neck. She had always hated the cold linoleum floor of that bathroom, but now her feet accepted the cold gratefully. Slowly, Autumn felt her strength returning.

"That's enough," she whispered, turning away from the faucet and resting her back against the tub. Icarus shut off the water. Autumn's head throbbed and her stomach did not cease its rebellion, but she felt remotely in control again.

"Can you walk?" Icarus asked.

Autumn nodded. She wasn't sure as her mind was preoccupied trying to convince her body not to start dry heaving again. He helped her up and peeked out the bathroom door.

"All clear," he said.

They crossed back to her bedroom and she toppled back into the bed, pushing the blankets as far away from her as possible.

"Here," Icarus said, and lifted a glass of water to her lips. "Sip it slowly."

Autumn took two, big, refreshing gulps. The water passed through her lips with such a gratifying sensation, but as it tried to settle in her stomach, she wished she had listened to Icarus. She curled into the fetal position, exhausted. Then she slipped into a dreamless sleep.

Chapter 11

Autumn awoke to the popping and rumbling of the neighbor's lawnmower. She cursed. Her head still throbbed, though her stomach felt a little better. She rolled over and checked her alarm clock on her nightstand. The bright, red digital numbers read ten fifteen AM. She had to get up. If she slept any longer it might arouse her family's suspicions. She hardly ever slept past nine.

She sat up and swung her feet off the bed. She sat holding her head in her hands and giving her mind a minute to orient itself. She had never thought that thinking could hurt, but somehow it did. The clearer she kept her mind, the less it hurt. But she had too many questions and too much to do. She walked over to her dresser, almost afraid to glance into the mirror. A greenish face with pitiful eyes stared back at her. She realized she still wore the sundress from the night before.

Then she remembered the party.

She slipped into the bathroom and took a shower, hoping that it would help. She felt a little bit better. She returned to her room and put on shorts and a tank-top. Then she sat down in front of the mirror and began to put on a thin layer of foundation to mask the green color.

She went downstairs, trying not to hold her head as she descended into her family's chaos.

On Saturdays, her father always ate lunch at home to spend time with the children. He sat at the table in his grease-stained blue shirt that had his name stitched on the left breast pocket. Autumn's mother stood by the island countertop preparing sandwiches for them all. Mikayla and Joey were arguing whether or not *The Lion, the Witch, and the Wardrobe* was the best book in *The Chronicles of Narnia*. The book was too advanced for Joey's reading level, but her family had played the audiobook in the car on their last vacation. Gracie sat next to Joey in silence.

Her father glanced over at her as she entered.

"Good morning, honey."

"It's closer to afternoon," her mother commented, without looking up.

"Did you sleep ok?" her father asked.

Autumn froze. Did he know? Or did she just look that bad in spite of trying to cover up how rough she felt? He couldn't know - they had been so careful when they left. Then it hit her that she couldn't remember how she had gotten back into bed. She could have come in like an elephant, for all she knew.

She sat down next to him at the table.

"Fine, thanks," she lied, resting her head in her hands. She had to talk to Icarus of all people, and he wasn't in the kitchen.

"Where's the new guy?" she asked.

"He went out for the morning," her mother said, glancing at the clock. "He should be home soon though."

Autumn closed her eyes for a moment, and then realized that Meghan and Ian would have answers. She slipped her cell phone out of her pocket. Ten missed texts and two missed phone calls, all from Meghan.

She unlocked her phone and skimmed through them.

8:45 AM   **Hey! are you alive?**
9:00 AM   **We need to talk!**

9:01 AM	Last night was epic!
9:01 AM	Can you meet us at mall around 1?
9:30 AM	Hello!?!?!
10:00 AM	Answer me!!!

"Autumn, you know the rules about phones at the table," her mother said.

She slid the phone back in her pocket, too distracted by the churning of her stomach and the ringing in her head to care or defend herself. She looked at the floor, wondering for a moment if she would throw up again.

"Are you sure you're ok?" her dad asked, as her mother put down a ham and cheese sandwich in front of him and then another in front of Autumn.

"I'm fine," she repeated, annoyed.

She took a bite of her sandwich and instantly realized she would never be able to stomach the whole thing. She got up and poured herself a tall glass of water and began sipping it slowly.

"Can you give me a ride to the mall, Mom? Meghan and Ian want to meet up for a bit."

A look passed between her mother and father, and Autumn feared her sneaking out might not have been as sneaky as she had thought. Her father nodded and her mother agreed. Maybe she would have to talk to Icarus after all.

"Sure. When Icarus gets back."

Autumn stayed quiet for the remainder of lunch. She didn't want to talk to Icarus; not until she knew more. She excused herself and asked her mom to let her know when they could leave.

She returned to her room and fought the urge to lay back down in bed and go to sleep. Instead, she went to her desk and took out her writing notebook, documenting anything she could remember, including the sensations in her stomach and head. Whether it was source material for her novel or simply an exercise to help her keep her sanity, she wasn't sure.

Chapter 12

Autumn looked up from her writing notebook at the sound of a car door. She went to her window, and saw the van back in the driveway and Icarus walking towards the house. She sat back at her desk and rested her head in her hands, waiting for her mother to come and get her.

"Are you ok?" Her mother asked.

Autumn lifted her head in a daze. She hadn't heard her mother come up the stairs.

"I'm fine," Autumn lied again.

"Are you sure you don't want to stay home and rest?"

Autumn forced herself to her feet. Why should she need rest?

"No, I just didn't sleep well. You know how it can be." Autumn regretted the awkward comment and hoped her mother wouldn't press the issue.

To her surprise, her mother didn't. She nodded and said. "Ok, well, I'll be in the van."

Autumn followed.

Neither talked on the drive to the mall. Autumn tried to keep her eyes open and her stomach in place. When they arrived, her mother dropped her at the Macy's entrance and told her that she would be back in an hour.

Autumn walked through the mall, her head still throbbing, and she began to regret the whole endeavor. But she needed answers, answers her friends could give her. She knew she had danced with Derek and they had kissed. *No, I dreamt the kiss. I dreamt the whole thing? How did I get home? Why was Icarus in my room when I woke up?*

She stopped so suddenly that the man behind her almost bumped into her. He stepped past her deliberately, muttering under his breath.

She had been so focused on Derek and the party that this new question began to eat her alive. Why had Icarus been there when she woke up? *Did we...? No. No, that can't be right.* The pain in her head increased as she tried to remember.

The buzzing of her cell phone in her hand caught her attention.

"Hello," she answered.

"Wow, someone is grumpy!" Meghan's voice boomed through the phone.

Autumn pulled the phone away from her ear before easing it back and answering.

"I just really don't feel well. Where are you guys?"

"Food court. Come meet us."

"Absolutely not. Too loud."

"Oh, rocking the hangover, huh? Alright, let's meet at Dunk's."

"Sure. Bye."

Autumn hung up and began walking again. She didn't have to look at the directory. Out of the few times she had come to the mall, Dunkin Donut's remained the only store she visited every single time. Not so much for her, but for her mother. Autumn didn't really like coffee, but at this point, she figured it couldn't hurt. She ordered a medium hot coffee with two creams and two sugars just as her mother always did. She took one sip and realized that it would be the only sip. She took the coffee and found a booth in the corner to wait for her friends.

A few minutes later, Ian and Meghan walked through

the door. Meghan looked to be her usual bubbly self, Ian a bit more the way Autumn felt.

"Hey girl!" Meghan exclaimed as she slipped into the booth.

"Finally!" Autumn said, beginning to feel irritated in her desperation.

"How was your night?" Ian asked with a wicked look in his eyes.

"Yeah, deets!" Meghan demanded.

"Actually, I was hoping you guys could tell me," Autumn said, trying to sound nonchalant about the whole affair.

Ian and Meghan's faces did not comfort her.

"You blacked out?" Meghan asked.

"Yeah," Autumn admitted

"Congratulations! My girl! I'm so proud of you!" Ian joked.

"Wait," Megan said. "What's the last thing you remember?"

"I was dancing with Derek and I think maybe we kissed?" Autumn said, adding more skepticism to her voice than she actually felt.

"Oh Megs, she doesn't remember," Ian said.

"Remember what?" Autumn asked.

"Well, um... so you and Derek did kiss-" Meghan began before Ian interrupted.

"More like made out hard!"

Meghan shot a side glance to Ian, who put his hands up in a gesture of surrender.

"I made out with Derek?" Autumn asked in disbelief. She couldn't help but smile. She tried desperately to remember it, but nothing surfaced. "I actually kissed Derek." She whispered, her fingers subconsciously touching her lips.

"That's not all..." Meghan said.

"What do you mean that's not all?" Autumn laughed. "That's huge! I mean it's not like we-"

She stopped. The brief memory of being carried upstairs flashed through her mind.

"Megs?" She began, but found she couldn't finish the question.

Meghan looked to Ian and he offered a simple nod of support.

"You and Derek went upstairs," Meghan began, "Then Icarus went up and came out with you. You could barely stand. He practically carried you to the van. Derek followed him, swearing up a storm. After Icarus buckled you in the back, he whipped around and clocked Derek hard."

Autumn couldn't believe it.

"He punched Derek?"

"Just once," Ian clarified. "But it was like a direct hit, feet up in the air type deal."

Autumn stared at her gross coffee.

I kissed Derek, she thought, but it didn't feel like a victory. A memory flashed of a bedroom ceiling. Her thoughts were like a thick fog as she desperately tried to remember. Derek had laid her on the bed. Had she told him she wanted to go back to her friends? *Why did I get so drunk?* Icarus had been there telling her they had to leave. *No... telling Derek.* Icarus had sworn at him. Her head rang like a snare drum.

Autumn stood up. "Where were you guys?" she demanded, but before her friends could answer, she turned and stormed out of the Dunkin Donuts. Meghan tried to follow, but Ian stopped her.

She needed to get out of the mall, the state, her life. She headed straight for the mall entrance before remembering she needed to text her mother to come pick her up. Feeling frustrated and exposed, she began to cry. She headed to the bathroom and sat in the stall for almost ten minutes before she got her tears under control. Feeling sick to her stomach and exhausted, she texted her mother and waited.

Her mother finally texted her that she was outside the Macys entrance, waiting in the fire lane. Autumn did her best to dry her eyes and headed to the door.

As she got to the passenger side door and opened it, her mother took one look at her and asked the question Autumn had prayed she wouldn't.

"Honey, what's wrong?"

And just like that, all of the emotional barriers Autumn had put up broke. One tear slipped out, like a leak in a dam, collapsing all of her defenses. Autumn wept.

Chapter 13

As soon as Autumn broke down, her mother pulled into the nearest parking space and ushered her through the van into the back seat. She hugged Autumn while the tears continued to fall.

Autumn knew her parents were strict, but she also knew neither had been saints in their youth. She hoped they would remember that. She had needed advice before, but not for anything so serious. With only two weeks before the end of high school, when had her world decided to come crashing down around her?

Her mother would need an explanation for the tears and Autumn debated what was safer, to tell her the truth or a lie?

When she could finally speak, Autumn told her mother everything that had happened, and to her surprise, the first words out of her mother's mouth weren't "You're grounded." She had sat there patiently, waiting for Autumn to finish her story.

"Your father and I aren't idiots. I know a hangover when I see one," Her mother began. "We also heard the van starting up when you two left last night."

Autumn felt her face turning red with embarrassment.

"You didn't say anything," Autumn commented.

"Another few months, and we will have very little say," her mother answered. "You will be away at college. You will have to make your own choices and be ready to accept the consequences."

It had seemed so appealing to Autumn only a few days ago, and now she began to wonder if she actually was ready for such a big step.

"Are you mad?" Autumn asked.

"Well, your father wanted to get the shotgun and chase after you two, but I calmed him down." She paused for a moment before continuing. "No, I'm not mad at you, I'm - I'm sorry it wasn't the night you had hoped for."

Autumn didn't even want to think about the inevitable conversation with her father. "What should I do?" she asked her mom.

Her mother thought for a moment.

"I can take you to the hospital, and they can do some tests to see if Derek raped you," She said, finally.

Autumn cringed at the thought.

"I think I want to talk to Icarus first. I think he knows what actually happened," she said, embarrassed.

"Ok," her mom answered.

Autumn watched the numbers on the dashboard clock change as they sat in silence. The minivan had become a peaceful little cocoon, protecting her from the chaos of the world, though Autumn doubted that she would turn into a beautiful butterfly when she emerged. She wished she could stay in the van, with her mom and the silence, but she knew she still had to face her father and Icarus.

"Can we go home now?" Autumn asked, after a few minutes.

"Of course," Her mother said, and made her way back to the front seat.

Autumn got out of the van and went around to the driver's side door, and the two embraced.

I love you, mom."

Chapter 14

Her mother didn't bring it up again for the rest of the ride home, and Autumn appreciated that. They did, however, make an "emergency ice cream" stop at Autumn's favorite little shop called *The Scoop*.

The whole ride home she had been dreading seeing Icarus. He had only known her for a few days, and he had already seen the worst parts of her life. He had been there, either watching her or watching over her. She walked into the kitchen and saw him at the table helping her little brother with math homework, his back to her.

"Hi, Autumn!" Joey said.

Icarus turned.

"Hi, Joey," she answered. "Icarus."

He smiled and nodded his acknowledgment. Then he turned back to Joey and they continued to do math.

He had looked at her so casually. So blasé. *He must think I'm a whore.* For a second, she thought she might cry again. She spoke before her tears could get the better of her.

"Icarus…can we go for a walk?"

"Sure," he answered before telling Joey, "Keep going. I'll check it later. Don't forget to carry your ones."

They both walked out the back door, and headed down the driveway towards the street.

The summer air was warm, but not hot. The sun beat down, but a refreshing breeze would pick up now and then to break it up. Their neighbor, Mr. Thomson, had finished mowing his lawn, and the smell of gasoline and fresh-cut grass filled the air.

"I need to ask you about last night," she said, staring at the ground, unable to look him in the eyes. "I don't remember anything."

"Yeah. You were pretty wrecked. You blacked out, not surprising. How much did you drink?"

"Not much, just a few glasses of that punch," she lied.

Icarus laughed. "You know the stuff in the punch is the strongest, right? You should have grabbed a beer."

Autumn shrugged. The information would be useful later, but didn't help her present situation.

"So what happened?" She pressed.

"You and Derek kissed. He brought you upstairs. I followed. I brought you back downstairs and we left."

He said it all matter-of-factly. Autumn appreciated that he didn't embellish on her, but he still hadn't answered her question. She had already known all of that.

"I meant more what happened in the bedroom?"

"Nothing happened."

A wave of relief swept over Autumn.

"But Derek tried," Icarus continued, "When I got to the bedroom, you were on the bed and he had just gotten his pants off. You were practically asleep."

Autumn cringed as he recounted the events of the prior night, she felt both terrified and grateful that she could not remember.

"Thank you," she said.

He gave a simple nod.

Her next question surprised her. It just slipped out.

"Do you think I'm pretty?"

His answer surprised her more.

"I think you are beautiful."

"I feel gross," she said. *Dirty* is what she meant. Not because she thought sex was dirty; she didn't, but for some reason, this whole situation seemed to have a filth she couldn't wash away.

Whether or not Icarus understood what she meant, he simply replied. "Sleep. It's the best cure I've found for a hangover. You'll feel better tomorrow."

She smiled.

"How did you know that would work?" she asked. "How did you know Derek would talk to me?"

"Basic human psychology. I upstaged the king. The king notes his enemies. I had three other girls in front of me, but I kept my arm around you, showing him that you were the prize."

"Oh, I'm a prize?" she asked, condescension in her tone.

"Like I said; psychology. I didn't say you had to like it."

"So you were a party goer?" she asked.

"I saw it in a movie once... I always wondered if it would work."

Autumn stopped, staring at him in disbelief, and she could tell by his laughter it was true. He had completely gambled.

He motioned for her to cross to the other side of the road with him, and they began to walk back towards the bed and breakfast. Icarus reached into the side pocket of his cargo shorts and produced a small book, a copy of *Odd Thomas* by Dean Koontz, which he handed over to her.

"I figured you might like this, I picked it up this morning."

He bought her a book. A man after her own heart.

"Thanks," she said. "How did you know I liked to read?"

"You assumed I was writing a book last night, and I noticed the bookshelf in your bedroom," he said. "Nice little graveyard you've got going on there."

"Excuse me?" she asked.

"Think about it, when you go to a graveyard you see tombstones right? And on each stone, there is a name and one or two sentences trying to sum up that person's life."

"Ok."

"When you go to a library you see the same thing; a little tombstone with a name."

He pointed to the big letters that read *Dean Koontz*.

"But then you open it and you get a glimpse into who that person is...what they struggled with, how they dealt with the world. Their lives. Their personal discoveries," he continued.

The rose-tinted glasses began to slip away, and he once more became the Icarus Falls she had first thought him to be, just as strange as his name.

"When you read a book, you can meet someone dead or alive. All of the knowledge in the world is passed down in books," he finished.

She smiled and shook her head. He was weird, but he was kind of cute and he had bought her a book. Her smile faded as they approached her home and saw her father waiting on the front porch. He stood leaning against the banister, clearly waiting.

"You kids mind if I talk to you for a sec?" he asked, as they approached.

Autumn almost wished the alcohol had just killed her.

Chapter 15

A s they walked up the stairs to the front porch, Autumn heard the wood groan beneath their weight, as if it too knew what was coming.

"Thanks for the walk," she said, motioning Icarus to the door.

"Oh no, I want to talk to you too. Have a seat," Her father interjected, and motioned to the porch swing.

Autumn cringed. Technically a love seat, the swing only had enough room for two people to sit very close together. Her father had installed it when the family moved in, and he and his wife had been known to sit and watch the sunset together from time to time.

"Dad, I-"

"Sit down," He commanded.

Autumn sat on the swing, shoulder to shoulder with Icarus. She had never had a partner in crime; she couldn't tell if she found his touch comforting or just awkward.

They both waited in silence as Autumn's father paced back and forth.

"Your mother and I have talked," he began, coming to a halt.

They waited for him to continue, but he simply returned to pacing.

Autumn shot a sideways glance at Icarus. He sat at attention, waiting patiently, a blank look on his face as if he were a soldier awaiting orders, or maybe chastisement.

"First, and I want you to think really hard before answering, what did you learn from this… escapade?"

Autumn waited for Icarus to answer, but he remained silent.

"I learned not to drink," Autumn answered, hoping that was what her father wanted to hear.

"I'm not stupid." He almost spat. "I know you will drink again. I want you to not drink too much."

Autumn remained silent, not knowing what to say.

"And if you are going to a party, I want you to be with people you can trust! People who won't leave you alone with strange boys, or let you get hurt in any other way."

Her father sighed and Autumn watched him go through what appeared to be the five stages of grieving in only a few seconds. His shoulders slouched as if all of the anger had exhausted him and now drained from his body. She had only seen her father cry once, at her grandfather's funeral, but now she feared he might cry again.

"Next year you will be going to college, and your mother and I won't be there. We will only be a phone call away," he added quickly, "but you will have to make your own decisions. Your mother and I have raised you as best we can and I know that that will stick with you. I also know that sometimes you will have to make your own mistakes. All I ask is that you *learn* from them, and please know that your mother and I love you no matter what."

Confusion wrapped itself around Autumn's head like a blanket. She wasn't sure if she should cry, thank him, or rejoice.

"Which brings me to my second point," he continued. "I should ground you for the disobedience *and* for stealing our van, which you technically *did*, and is no small offense… but I think you have been through enough."

Autumn sat speechless.

"If you want to press charges against that boy, Derek,

you let me know. I'm going to call his parents either way, but I don't want to make this a public affair without your approval."

Autumn always knew her parents loved her but the way her father looked at her as he finished speaking said much more than any simple I love you.

Autumn stood and hugged him, just as she had embraced her mother.

When she was a little girl, she had loved being held by her father. She couldn't remember the last time she had hugged him. When she finally let him go, she saw him brush a tear out of his watery eyes.

"You can go," he said, quietly; gesturing towards the door.

As Autumn opened the screen door, she looked at Icarus, waiting.

"You, on the other hand," her father said, looking at Icarus. "We need to talk."

The heat in the house made Autumn feel sick again, and knowing she no longer needed to keep up the façade with her parents, she went back to bed.

Chapter 16

When Autumn's mother came into her room on Sunday morning to wake her for church, Autumn felt much better. The pain in her head had finally gone, and her stomach had more or less settled. She figured she would be fine, so long as she didn't eat any spicy food for a while.

She went to her closet and dressed. She felt that she had outgrown church about a year ago, but her mother had not given her much of a choice. Apparently, if Autumn stopped going, it would raise questions with the younger children. At the end of the day, Mass only lasted an hour and it gave Autumn time to go over her stories in her head, filling in holes in the plotlines and planning more adventures, while Father Patrick blathered on about how the world was off to hell in a handbasket.

They had breakfast, piled into the van, and left for church. Autumn felt relieved to see that Icarus had not been kicked out of the family. They sat together in the backseat of the minivan with Gracie. Joey had been gracious enough to switch with Autumn and sit in the seat next to Mikayla.

Autumn slipped out her phone and opened a notepad. She typed:

Glad to see you're still with us.

Icarus smiled.

Autumn wondered if his conversation had been that easy with her father. Had he just smiled his charming Icarus Falls smile and it had all been fine? She doubted it.

When they arrived at the church, her family filed out of the van, and upon entering, found a seat somewhere in the middle of the pews. Autumn had hoped to sit next to Icarus, but they had gotten separated by the children, and now she sat between Mikayla and her parents.

The service began.

Autumn tended to lose interest in Mass after the first five minutes, and then would try to devote the rest of her time to her stories; refining plotlines, imagining new characters, etc. She wondered if she would attend church in college. She didn't particularly enjoy it or feel it necessary, but it had been a part of her life for so long, she had a hard time imagining not going. It held a strange sense of familiarity. She would love to skip, but similarly to school, she couldn't help but question if it did help her on some subconscious level.

Autumn looked at the tall gothic arches and the thin stain-glassed windows. A cathedral modeled church, it reminded her of *The Hunchback of Notre Dame* by Victor Hugo. She had often passed the time at church imagining herself as Esmerelda, a poor gypsy girl who sought sanctuary from an evil man and met another unique one. In her version, it morphed a bit. The hunchback turned out to be a prince in disguise and he would rescue her. As she grew older, her version had felt stupider and stupider; she didn't want to be rescued anymore. Her eyes moved down from the high arching ceilings until they fell upon Icarus.

He listened attentively to the priest, his back straight and his eyes locked on Father Patrick with that weird Icarus Falls intensity. He appeared as if he were waiting or expectant, like he had a question burning in the back of his mind, and he believed the answer would be revealed if he just watched someone long enough.

What is that question? Autumn wondered.

Autumn watched him for the rest of the Mass, careful not to be caught by him or any other member of her family. He seemed almost familiar with the service, but he didn't sing along with any of the songs, so perhaps she was wrong. Even the people she knew who couldn't sing usually slipped up at some point and mouthed the words. Icarus did not.

After Mass, they all drove back in the mini-van; her mom and dad in the front, the children in the back, and she and Icarus Falls in the middle.

Sundays were family days, and her dad didn't work on any cars. He chose to spend more of the day with his wife and kids than just dinner. They all would come home from church as a family, and after lunch, they would play board games together.

Her father went to the fridge and pulled out a Sam Adams. He wasn't much of a drinker, but he reserved the right to have a beer or two on Sunday afternoons and holidays. He took out a second, which he offered to Icarus.

"No one should have to drink alone," Icarus stated, clinking the neck of his bottle against her father's.

Autumn's stomach churned and she had to look away. Just the sight of the beer made her feel sick.

She wondered why her father would let Icarus drink in their house, and she realized that Icarus must be twenty-one. She tried to recall if he had ever stated his age and wondered how her father knew. *The license and registration for the car.* The two things the police always asked for, as did her father when he worked on out-of-state cars.

Icarus is twenty-one.

The doorbell rang a second time before Autumn heard it. Her mother had begun preparing lunch and was rummaging through the fridge, while her father directed the children to the dining room.

"Can someone get that?" her mother asked, but Autumn knew she really meant *Autumn, could you get that.*

"Yup," she answered, as she headed down the hall to the front door.

Chapter 17

S he opened the door to find a young man not much older than herself.

He wore thin-rimmed glasses and his eyes seemed to squint, whether from the glasses or his smile, Autumn couldn't tell. His beard, or rather scruff that would presumably someday become a beard, jutted out unkempt, and he wore a black wife-beater tank top which contrasted with his painfully white skin.

Autumn's eyes shifted to the girl next to him. Her shoulder-length hair hung like a curtain, over one eye. Its black and blue tint complimented her mesmerizing green eyes. She had an athletic, toned body, and her bronze skin with patches of tattoos gave her a rather exotic look. She wore a royal blue spaghetti strap tank top that Autumn's mother never would have let Autumn wear, with white jean shorts. In her arms she held the happiest looking little baby.

The baby looked at Autumn from his perch, reaching out with his chubby little arm and gurgling.

"Is this the B&B?" the young man asked.

"Well hello there!" Autumn's mother said, stepping out of the doorway from behind Autumn. "Oh, Autumn, I forgot to tell you we have late arrivals today."

"Apparently," Autumn said to nobody in particular.

"I'm Kurt, this is Destiny," the young man said.

"Welcome," Autumn's father said, stepping out onto

the porch. "I hear congratulations are in order?"

"Thanks, man! It's crazy! I can't believe we're married."

Honey-mooners, Autumn thought, before wondering why anyone would choose to come to New Hampshire for their honeymoon.

"And what is your name?" Autumn's mother asked, scooping the baby up from his mother's arms.

"That's Scooter," Kurt answered proudly.

"Are you hungry?" Autumn's mother asked. "There is cereal, peanut butter, and jelly; I can make you eggs and toast if you'd like."

"I would love some cereal," Destiny said, her face lighting up with gratitude.

"PB&J would be great," Kurt said, before heading back to their car and grabbing their two suitcases.

"How long have you been married?" Destiny asked.

"Going on 20 years," Autumn's father answered.

"What's the secret?" Kurt asked, half-joking and half-serious.

"Communication," Autumn's mother said. "If you two can find your own way to not just talk, but really listen and respond, you'll be fine."

Autumn's mother led the way back to the kitchen, while her father directed Kurt to a room where he could leave their luggage.

As they entered the kitchen, the baby was passed to Autumn. Her mother went to work making an impromptu lunch, and peppering Destiny, who sat at the barstool, with a barrage of questions about Kurt, how the two had met, and their wedding.

Autumn hadn't been around a baby in a while, and she had to admit she enjoyed holding one again. She heard movement in the hallway, and turned to see Icarus walk in.

He waved to Scooter.

"Would you like to hold him?" Autumn asked.

"No."

"Oh, are you one of *those* guys?"

"What guys?" Icarus asked.

"Guys who are afraid of babies?" Autumn teased.

"Nope!" Icarus answered. "I can play peek-a-boo with the best of them. I just don't like holding things that can die if I drop them."

Autumn almost laughed at how ridiculous he sounded. She had never seen him out of his element.

He watched Autumn and the child from a safe distance.

"Where's my little man?" Kurt exclaimed, announcing his entrance into the kitchen. Autumn returned the baby to his father.

She glanced at Icarus. He watched the visitors with a strange gaze. She couldn't tell if it was with envy or confusion. He almost looked as though he wanted nothing more than to understand them. *What was he looking for?* His eyes moved over Kurt and the baby and finally settled on Destiny. There it was again. The Icarus Falls stare. It wasn't a creepy up down that many guys would give; it was an intense eye contact that seemed to be almost soul searching. Autumn had never realized just how dangerous that stare could be. It looked as if Icarus was aiming a precision laser.

Destiny caught his gaze and shifted uncomfortably in her chair.

Just like that, it was over. He no longer held an interest in them. Autumn felt as if she were watching a movie where two characters knew something that the audience didn't.

She began to wonder about the tiny family which had found their way into her family's kitchen. What was their story? Their age suggested they had been high school sweethearts. Autumn looked at the tattoos on the girl's arm. There was a phoenix on her shoulder and an arrow between her thumb and forefinger. She had heard that most tattoos held meaning and she wondered what these meant.

Autumn looked back to Icarus, who had turned to leave. Autumn gave him a few seconds head start before following him. She found him on the front porch, sitting back in the loveseat swing.

"You'll make a good mother someday," he said.

"Who says I want to be a good mother?" Autumn countered.

"Are you asking who says you want to be a mother? Or who says you want to be a *good* mother?" He laughed, clearly back in his comfort zone.

"I *want* to be a writer," she said, a hint of defiance in her tone.

"You can be a writer and a mother."

Autumn ignored the comment. "What about you?"

"When I was a kid, I wanted to be a superhero," he said.

"Get out!"

"I'm serious. I couldn't read full sentences until the fourth grade. My parents bought me comic books, hoping that more pictures and fewer words would help."

Icarus looked over to see Autumn's face.

"What?" He asked.

"Oh, I'm just imaging tiny Icarus running around with a little cape, fighting bad guys."

"You laugh, but I'm still torn up about the fact it didn't work out."

"Well, you got to punch at least one bad guy."

"I suppose I did," he said, looking at her.

She leaned up against the porch rail.

"What do you think makes a person a villain?" he asked her.

She pondered his question recalling her vast inventory of evil literary figures such as; Mr. Hyde, Professor Moriarty, and Dorian Gray.

Intention? She wondered.

"Hey, guys! Am I interrupting something?" Mike asked.

He had walked all the way up the front lawn and Autumn hadn't even noticed him.

"Not at all," Icarus said.

"I don't believe we've met," Mike said, extending his hand.

"Icarus."

"I'm Mike. Icarus, that's a unique name."

"Well, it's not as commonplace as Mike."

"He's the new family chauffeur," Autumn said, not enjoying this interaction at all.

"I see," said Mike.

Autumn looked at him expectantly. She didn't know how to gracefully ask 'why are you here?' without sounding rude.

"Mom sent me over to see if she could borrow a cup of sugar," Mike clarified.

Ever since Autumn could remember, Mike's mom had always needed a cup of sugar when baking banana bread. She figured it was a ploy between their mothers to get her and Mike to spend more time together, but to be fair it was, in Autumn's opinion, the world's greatest banana bread.

"Mom's in the kitchen," Autumn said.

"The kitchen, right. Which one is that again?" Mike asked.

Autumn knew he had intended the remark to sound clever and witty, but it hadn't. He sounded like a desperate idiot.

Icarus didn't bother to suppress his grin.

"Come on," Autumn said, and led Mike into the kitchen.

Chapter 18

Autumn reasoned that Mike's mother couldn't have needed a cup of sugar all that badly, as she watched the numbers on the digital clock on the stovetop change from one to the next. Mike had gotten the cup of sugar right after he met Destiny and Kurt, and held the baby until they politely excused themselves. Now, Autumn watched as Mike still stood in the kitchen, chatting it up with her father. She found it quite comical, watching Mike hold a cup of sugar in his hand while he talked as her father held a beer. If he wasn't careful, he might actually forget and take a sip.

"Will you be joining us for games?" Autumn's mother asked, as she brought in a stack of board games and cards and placed them on the table.

Mike looked at the cup of sugar, then to the table, then to Autumn.

"I should probably get this back," he admitted.

Autumn shifted towards the table as Mike said his goodbyes. He came to her last, as he always did, and gave her a hug.

Once Mike had left, Autumn's family all took their places at the table and began their Sunday afternoon game tradition.

They played an aggressive game of Uno, and despite all the questions that flooded Autumn's mind, she inevitably found that her competitive streak won out. After Uno, they played Pokeno, a Bingo-like game which had been passed down by Autumn's grandmother. Autumn remembered playing for penny prizes at Thanksgiving and Christmas when her grandmother had been alive. She also noticed that Icarus Falls seemed to be helping Gracie to win.

The realization that she would miss it caught her off guard. Not everyday life, but Sundays. She looked around the table at her family. They had almost driven her to the edge of sanity over the past eighteen years, but they were what she had been given, and she loved them more than anything else in the world. She knew Meghan and Ian would keep in touch and eventually she would find someone to settle down with, but the five people right in front of her would always hold a special place in her heart. She began to question why she picked a college so far away. Then, she remembered she had to go back to school in only a matter of hours.

This occupied her mind all through dinner. Not her family, not Icarus Falls, but school. How would she face her friends? Her peers? All the strangers who had witnessed her folly?

After dinner, the family went into the living room to watch one episode of Gilligan's Island, the old TV show from the seventies. Her father had loved it as a boy, and due to the random nature of the show, had learned a lot of trivia which drove her mother crazy, and had become the main reason they played no trivia-based games.

After that, her father and mother prepped for Monday morning, while the kids got ready for bed.

Autumn brushed her teeth and changed into her PJs, dreading going back to school. As she laid in bed waiting for her parents to say goodnight, she picked up the book *Odd Thomas* and lost herself in a world far better than this one.

A gentle knock pulled her from the story. Her mother stood in the doorway, in her PJs.

"Where did you get that?" she asked, entering and sitting on the edge of the bed.

"Icarus got it for me," Autumn answered.

Her mother took the book and examined it.

"Hmm, Koontz – he has good taste. Koontz isn't as gross as Stephen King."

"No one is better than Stephen King," Autumn laughed. "You read stuff like this?"

"Occasionally," her mother smiled, "Just don't let the little ones know."

Autumn smiled for a moment. Then she remembered that she would soon be back at school. Her smile faded.

"Are you ok, sweetie?" her mother asked.

"Yeah," she answered. "I talked to Icarus... he got there in time."

Her mother remained silent, letting Autumn run the conversation, but Autumn could see her mother's relief.

"I don't know what to do tomorrow," Autumn confessed.

"Go to school and don't take shit from anyone," her mother stated, without missing a beat.

"Mom!" Autumn laughed.

Her mother smiled.

"Can I say that now?"

"Absolutely not," her mother said, kissing Autumn on the forehead. Then she rose and went to the door.

"Whatever they say, you know who you are."

"Do I?" Autumn asked.

"Yeah... You do," Her mother said, turning out the light.

Chapter 19

Monday morning arrived with its typical chaos. Autumn had been up until almost three AM, her mind a maze of scenarios of what the following day might bring. She knew she would have to go back to school. She would have to face everyone. She would have to face Derek. In the moments she did manage to forget all of the potential mayhem Monday could bring, she did not find peace. Instead, her mind began to try to puzzle together a new mystery; who was Icarus Falls?

She had gone over every interaction in her mind, from the day she had met him to the night he had saved her. She realized she really didn't know much of anything about him. She had sat up in bed with her secret penlight between her teeth, writing a list of questions in her notebook.

Her questions about Icarus and concerns about returning to school had kept her up until exhaustion had finally smothered her to sleep.

"Autumn, the toast is burning!" Gracie exclaimed.

Autumn came back to her senses. It felt as if she had woken up underwater. Her motions were almost as slow as her thoughts. The eggs were scrambled and would soon be overcooked, and the toast which she had pushed down for a second time, started to give off the acrid odor of something burning.

Icarus stepped into the kitchen, and before Autumn could say anything, manually popped the toast. He put the black and charred pieces on a plate, slipped another two out of the loaf, inserted them into the toaster, and pressed it down.

Here he is again, Autumn mused. *Saving the day.*

"Thanks," Autumn said as she slid the scrambled eggs onto two plates and rinsed out the pan in the kitchen sink. Icarus flicked off the burner and brought both plates to the table.

"The toast will be along shortly, bud," he said to Joey as he put one of the plates in front of him. Then he returned to the toaster, telling Autumn to go start her breakfast as he passed her by.

She felt too tired to be agitated.

"What is that smell?" Mikayla asked as she entered, her hair still damp from the shower.

"Your toast!" Icarus exclaimed, holding out the two charred pieces to Mikayla.

"Gross," she replied, grabbing a bowl and walking over to the Cheerios and milk on the table.

Icarus proceeded to butter the blackened pieces and sat at the table. Autumn put the pan on the drying rack and opted for cereal as well.

"You're not gonna-" Gracie began, and Icarus took a big bite of the burnt buttered toast. All of the children gaped in amazement, and even Autumn's stomach churned a bit as they heard the loud crunching sound it made. He struggled to get it down but then said "delicious!" and took another bite as the children giggled.

As usual with Icarus, they were all somehow in the car on time.

Once they had dropped off the children, Autumn knew she only had ten minutes. Ten minutes before he dropped her off. Ten minutes to get answers. She tried to reach back into her mind for the questions from the night before, but most of the questions that lingered were about whether or not her social life would survive in ten minutes when she began her school day.

"So, what's your story?" Autumn asked.

"My story?"

"Yeah. Do you just drive around looking for weird families to fall in with?"

Icarus laughed. "No. No, I don't," he answered.

"So, not a serial killer?" she asked.

"First a vampire, now a serial killer. I'm not sure how I should take that," he said with a smile.

He had a nice smile.

"Do you have any siblings?" Autumn continued, trying to be more direct.

"No," he answered.

"Did you drop out of high school?"

"No."

The night before, Autumn had been willing to bet money he had.

"Are you running from something?" she asked.

Icarus paused. She had been right about something.

"I think leaving something might be a more accurate way of putting it," he answered.

He could call it whatever he wanted; she had been right.

"What do you like to do for fun?" she continued.

"Read."

"Favorite thing to read?"

"*The Highwayman*, Alfred Noles."

He put his blinker on and, after waiting for two cars to pass, pulled into the school drop off zone.

"Final question," he said, as he pulled up to the curb.

Autumn didn't hesitate. She would ask him the obvious question that had been in her mind since the day she had met him. It had been so subtle she hadn't noticed it at first.

"Is Icarus Falls your real name?"

He turned to her, and, looking her in the eyes answered, "No."

"What is your real name?" she asked.

He smiled again, but this time it was the smile he had used at the party. "I'm afraid you've used your last question."

"Oh, come on!" Autumn demanded.

"You're going to be late," he said.

She almost flicked him off, but chose to stick out her tongue instead.

She disembarked from the vehicle and followed the sidewalk up to the stone steps where her friends always waited for her before school.

They stood watching her as she approached.

"Hey," Meghan said, her face an open book of passive aggression.

Autumn looked at Ian, who pretended to answer a text. They had left things on bad terms.

"Megs... Ian," she began, not really knowing what to say, and hoping they would help her out.

Meghan glared at her.

Ian remained impassive.

"We are sorry for not being better friends and for not constantly babysitting you," Meghan finally stated.

Meghan had a point. Autumn's friends hadn't been there to protect her, but Autumn had been the one who had chosen to get drunk.

"I'm sorry I blew you two off, and didn't let you know I was ok," Autumn answered before adding, "and for hurting your fragile egos."

Meghan laughed lightly.

"Oh come on," Ian said, wrapping his arms around them both, and bringing them into a group hug that neither girl wanted. "But seriously, girl, we're sorry we didn't have your back at the party. But you scared the crap out of us at the mall!"

"I'm sorry," Autumn repeated, drying a tear.

Ian released them, and Autumn saw that Meghan had begun "ugly crying" as she called it. They both cracked up laughing as their tears continued to flow.

"Thanks, Ian; now we have to fix our make-up!" Megan whined.

"Oh, boo-hoo!" Ian laughed.

The girls dried their eyes and they all began to head to their first classes.

"You really ok?" Meghan asked.

"Yes," Autumn said, feeling her tears coming again but fighting them. "Can we just forget it?"

"Ok," Meghan said, "but only if you tell us about Icarus Falls."

"Oh gosh," Autumn groaned.

"Meghan, did you not see the 'look back' Autumn gave him this morning?" Ian asked. "I believe you and I are out of the running."

"I did not give him the look back!" Autumn exclaimed.

"Oh don't you play innocent! I know it when I see it! You stepped out of that mini-van, I counted to three, you looked back, and I'd have sworn you were Meg Ryan and he was Tom Hanks!"

"How about a reference from our time?" Meghan requested.

Ian scoffed, "You two have no appreciation for good cinema."

Chapter 20

Autumn sat in class, her head propped up on one hand, while the other doodled aimlessly in her notebook. She didn't have the attention span for whatever review her teacher was giving and she knew as long as she glanced at her notes before the final she would be fine. She had rekindled things with her friends and she hadn't run into Derek, which surprisingly hadn't been on her mind as much as she had thought it would. She struggled to keep her eyes awake while her teacher blathered on, and her mind continued to work on the problem of Icarus Falls.

It hadn't been a huge mystery that his name wasn't Icarus. She wondered who would name their kid Icarus, and then realized he had chosen the fake name for himself. She wrote the name down on the edge of her writing notebook, then went back to doodling.

She tried to remember the story of Icarus, and pondered why someone would take the name for an alias until the bell rang for lunch. She had almost shut the notebook when she remembered to also write down *The Highway Man* on the edge of the paper. She had never read it, but she would; or at least find a synopsis of it.

Autumn headed to the cafeteria, hoping to meet up with her friends and avoid anyone else. She didn't want to bump into Derek or Mike or really anyone. She walked with her head down as she pushed into the current of students passing through the halls, and wondered if this was what it was like to be paranoid.

As she entered the lunchroom she couldn't help but think of an action flick she had seen her dad watching in passing: a man had entered a prison cafeteria and punched out the first man who had given him crap. In a lot of ways, high school was like prison. You had a regulated schedule, limited time outside, and new people got picked on. She gritted her teeth and clenched her fist, though she felt relatively confident she would not need to punch anyone.

She grabbed a tray and got in line for the hot lunch. After receiving her portion, she started off in the direction of her friends' table. She had almost made it, when Shannon and her posse stopped her.

"Hey, Mary," Shannon said.

Autumn looked at her quizzically.

"Like Magdalena? The whore?" Shannon added. "Jeez, I thought you were a church girl!"

Autumn wondered how long Shannon had spent searching the internet for that insult. After all, Shannon was not a "church girl" and she had made that very clear on several occasions. Autumn glanced over at Meghan, who had left her seat and begun walking over to rescue her.

"What, nothing to say?" Shannon continued. "There's no knight in shining armor to save you now."

"Well, at least someone thought I was worth saving." Autumn had no idea where the words had come from, but they were met with a cold silence that could have been swept in on a breeze from Dante's ninth circle of hell.

Autumn knew the comment had been cruel, but again, like prison, she knew if she didn't stick up for herself she would get walked on. Autumn pushed by Shannon and headed to her friends, half expecting to have something hurled at the back of her head.

Shannon cursed under her breath.

Autumn walked up to Meghan, who had overheard the tail end of the conversation and stood gawking. Autumn ushered her back to their table with Ian.

As Autumn took her first bite of lunch, she saw Derek walk through the cafeteria doors. He had been kept late after a class. Their eyes met for a moment and he quickly looked away. He had nothing to say to her. Autumn would have felt relieved, if she had not been so distracted by his face. The area around his left eye looked black as an ink stain. She watched as he got his food and sat with his friends, his back to her.

"I don't think you need to worry about awkward conversation with that one," Ian commented. "Looks like you're just getting the cold shoulder till graduation."

"I'm fine with that," Autumn answered.

"You ok?" Meghan asked.

She thought about it. "Yeah," then added, "Wow, Icarus must really know how to throw a punch."

They all laughed a little.

"Word around school is Derek tripped coming down the stairs," Ian commented.

"Please! Like anyone believes that!" Meghan exclaimed.

"A mysterious boy, a fighter, the look back... what's going on with you two?" Ian asked.

"Nothing!" Autumn cried, but she couldn't keep a straight face. She could feel the heat as she began to blush.

"No fair! I called him!" Meghan retorted.

"Oh hush," Ian said.

Chapter 21

S tudy hall finally came, and Autumn asked her teacher to
be excused to go to the library for research. Mrs. Larson,
her teacher, permitted it. Not everyone could go to the library
during study hall; it depended on the teacher's mood, how
the class had been behaving in general, and who was asking.
Autumn had always been a good student and not one to abuse
her privileges.

Once she arrived, Autumn walked up to the library
computer and opened the internal library search engine. *This
is stupid,* she thought, as her finger rested over the enter key.
She looked once more over the name she had entered - *Icarus
Falls.* She pressed enter, and the loading circle began to spin.
Autumn had just moved the mouse to hover over the "cancel
search" button when one result came up. She frantically
reached for the mini pencil and sticky note that the library left
by the computers for people to write down reference numbers
of books they were looking for. She scratched it down quickly,
and then trying not to run, headed into the body of books. She
scanned as she went, until she found it. She slid the book off
of the shelf and stared at the cover.

The graveyard: a collection of poetry. Autumn read
the forward. Disappointment filled her when she learned it
had been part of an aspiring author's competition. There was
no way to know where each contributing author was from.

Poetry, she thought. She didn't know why, but Icarus

hadn't struck her as someone who would write that. She had figured he would be a poetic writer, but not an actual writer of poetry. She flipped to the page which had been listed next to his name in the table of contents.

Atlas – by Icarus Falls

Black and white mix to gray
and the ink begins to fade
They say the only cure is time
There is freedom in the grave
So take the world upon your shoulders
don't be frightened by the weight
Push your burden up the mountain
or stay here remain the slave
How much will you bear?
Can you show me that you care?
Can you say it? Look me straight in the face!

Will you rise or will you fall?
Never mind - just give your all!
Find the way out away from this place
Find your way out away from this place

The air is gone
A kiss so wrong
These lips were open all along
Only death will reveal your hearts beliefs
Come and gone
Now run along
Like verses stolen from a song
Steal your life back from the silent thief
Steal your life back from the silent thief

Autumns eyes scanned the words over and over. She couldn't help herself. The words captivated her and resonated in her heart. Like an insect in a flame, they burned her. *Who is he?* she thought. *Who is Icarus Falls?*

Autumn read the poem several times, until she could recite it back to herself. Then she slipped the book back into its resting place and returned to the computers. She typed in *The Highway Man* by Alfred Noyes. She stared at the screen skeptically as it displayed that the only available copy was a graphic novel.

She made her way over to her least favorite section of the library; the graphic novel section. Comic books and anime weren't good literature in her eyes, and she refused to waste her time reading them. She had enough social problems without being labeled a geek, nerd, or illiterate.

She found the book, and slipping it out of its spot on the shelf, began to thumb through the first few pages, not realizing just how easily she fell into it. The thin book had less than fifty pages, but those pages held a type of magic Autumn had never quite experienced. The noir style illustrations with their dramatic highlights and shadows enchanted her.

Another poem! she thought surprised.

The rustling of chairs snapped Autumn out of the trance. She glanced at one of the large clocks the school had installed on each of the major walls in the library, and realized she would have to borrow the book. Study hall was almost over.

As she brought it to the counter, she saw the school librarian, Ms. Stanwood.

Tall and slender with dark hair and eyes, Ms. Stanwood reminded Autumn of an old Victorian painting. Her features were not exotic, but she was a striking none the less. Too young to be a mother but too old to be a friend, the librarian always seemed to look a little out of place in the high school, and no matter where Autumn saw her, Ms. Stanwood always seemed to be reading a book.

Autumn had once seen the woman reading a copy of *Pride and Prejudice* in the cafeteria, and it had occurred to Autumn that if Mike had been several years older, they probably would have been the perfect couple.

"Good afternoon," Ms. Stanwood said, as Autumn put the book down on the desk.

"Hey," Autumn responded, her eyes shifting over to the clock.

"The Highway Man," Ms. Stanwood commented as she picked up the book and scanned in the barcode. "This is a great poem."

"You know it?"

"Of course! Haven't you seen *Anne of Green Gables*?"

Autumn shook her head.

"I suppose that is a bit before your time. Anyway, this will be due back on Monday, so don't forget about it over the weekend."

Autumn thanked her and turned to leave before she remembered something.

"Ms. Stanwood, you teach mythology, right?"

"Yes, to the ninth grade. Why?"

Autumn glanced at the clock, then back to the teacher.

"Do you know the story of Icarus?"

A girlish smile broke on the librarian's face.

"I've been hearing that name whispered a lot in the halls, lately," she commented with a hint of interest.

Autumn didn't bite.

After a moment of silence, Ms. Stanwood realized that she would not be receiving any information beyond what she had heard in whispers around the school, so she told Autumn the story of Icarus.

It was just as Autumn remembered; a kid who tried to

fly and drowned in the ocean.

"I don't understand," Autumn said. "It's just a crap story."

"Maybe it's not the story you should be focused on, but rather the lesson," Ms. Stanwood suggested.

"The lesson?"

"Yes. Most ancient stories have deeper meanings. Like Aesop's fables or even Grimm's fairytales...that is, before Disney got to them." Ms. Stanwood said, with a hint of disdain.

"What does the story of Icarus mean?" Autumn asked.

"What do you think it means?" The librarian countered.

Autumn felt like a burglar in someone's house as the owners pulled into the driveway. Her palms had begun to sweat as the clock continued to tick closer and closer to when the bell would ring.

"I don't know."

"Try." Ms. Stanwood said. It sounded a bit more like a command this time.

Screw it. Autumn thought about it. "Disobedience?"

Ms. Stanwood smiled.

"His father had warned him not to fly too close to the sun, but Icarus disobeyed, and he paid with his life," Autumn reasoned.

Why would someone take that name? *Someone who disobeyed. Icarus Falls has daddy issues?* She almost laughed at the thought.

"Thanks, Ms. Stanwood."

"Anytime. Is there anything else I can help you with today?"

"I'm good, thanks again," Autumn said, and she left.

Chapter 22

*D*isobedience.

Autumn pondered the word, wondering what it could mean for Icarus. Had he made a mistake and fallen away? And what about his poem, *Atlas*? It wasn't about disobedience. Autumn was so lost in thought as she walked back to study hall, she didn't see Mike come around the corner until she had almost walked by him.

"Autumn, are you ok?"

With all of the mayhem over the last few days between the party, Derek, and the prom - which was only a week and a half away and she would be more than happy to skip at this point – Autumn just wanted to go home and give up any social life she had until college. It had already been a long, emotional day, and she had no desire for verbal swordplay with Mike.

"I'm fine. Why wouldn't I be?" Autumn asked, wondering how he had escaped class until she saw the bathroom pass in his hand.

"I just heard what happened. You know...at the party," Mike whispered the last part.

Autumn looked away.

"I'm sorry, I would have said something yesterday, but I didn't know," he continued. "I wish I had been there."

Sure Mike, make this all about you, she thought.

"It's ok. I already had a knight in shining armor."

She regretted the words instantly. Though she didn't

see him in a romantic way, Mike had always been a good friend and had meant well. He looked at her a bit like a wounded puppy, scolded just for loving its master. *Strike two.* If she kept it up they wouldn't be friends at all. She tried to think of something to say, some way to backpedal. Then the bell rang.

"I have to go," he said and brushed by her.

Chapter 23

When the last bell rang, Autumn tried not to run down the hall to her locker. She switched books at her locker and said goodbye to her friends. She did not feel safe until she got into the minivan and shut the door, creating a physical barrier between herself and her high school.

"How was your day?" Joey asked from the back.

"Exhausting," she answered. "How about you?"

"Pretty good," he replied.

As they pulled away from the curb, she watched Mike walking to his car, clearly lost in thought. She shook her head in frustration. Why did things have to be so complicated with him? It all used to be so simple.

"Nice book you got there," Icarus said.

Autumn had forgotten to hide *The Highway Man* in her bag. She had held it close to her chest with her arms crossed as if had been a shield, or maybe a life preserver, as she made her way to the van. Now, it rested on her lap.

"What is it?" Joey asked.

"The Highway Man," Autumn answered. "It's a poem."

"What's it about?" Joey pressed.

Autumn looked to Icarus.

"I'll read it to you later if you want," Icarus offered.

"Are we going to understand it?" Mikayla asked, not looking up from her Sudoku. "Most poetry doesn't make much sense."

"You don't like poetry?" Icarus asked in disbelief.

None of the children denied it.

"Well, hopefully, this will act as a gateway then. It's easy to understand. Honestly, it's more of a short story."

"I didn't realize you were so into poetry," Autumn teased.

He glanced at her with a look she couldn't quite decipher.

They spent the rest of the ride home discussing Joey's day, and then Gracie's. Shy as Gracie was, she didn't seem to shy away from Icarus Falls. In fact, she probably talked to him more than she had to any other non-family member.

When they got home, the kids all went and did their Monday chores.

Icarus held Autumn back and asked how her day was. She admitted to the one incident with Shannon, which Icarus found amusing. Then, she went on to do her chores as well.

When she finished, she found Icarus in the living room with her brother and sisters, reading *The Highway Man*. She waited in the doorway like a ghost of the house, not wishing to disturb them. He charmed each of them as he spoke each word and carefully turned each page.

After several minutes, she left for her room. She needed some time to herself before dinner. Normally she would have sat on the porch with a book, but it had begun to rain and she felt the urge to write anyway. She sat down at her desk and opened her notebook, looking at the column labeled "relevant". She wrote down the word "disobedient" followed by "daddy issues". Then she wrote down "highwayman". She thought about it for a minute. She tried envisioning him as the highwayman in the poem and laughed. He would drive all night to get to her window. She shook her head, trying to erase the distraction as if her mind was an etch a sketch. *Could it be a metaphor? Because he drove on the highway? He's a highway driving poet who had had a falling out with his father...over what?* She wondered.

Her mother called her for dinner, and she shut the notebook and headed downstairs to her place at the table. They said the blessing and Autumn felt content, until her father said the words she hadn't expected to hear.

"Well, Icarus, I finally got around to finishing out those repairs today. Your car should easily have another fifty thousand miles in it if you take care of her."

"It's good to drive?" Icarus asked.

"Good as new," her father answered.

"I can't tell you how grateful I am for everything."

No, Autumn thought.

"I guess I will head out in the morning then," he said.

"Where to?" her mother asked.

To his love. She didn't know where the thought had come from, but it disturbed her. If he had been in love, he wouldn't have left to come out to the middle of nowhere, would he? No, that wasn't it, and she hadn't done it yet. She hadn't solved the mystery of Icarus Falls. She had to stop him from leaving, she was so close.

"I want you to take me to prom," Autumn blurted out.

Chapter 24

Autumn's grandfather, a WWII veteran, had been a paratrooper and had once told her, "The first time you jump out of an airplane to parachute, you have one thought: 'Oh crap, why did I just jump out of a perfectly good airplane?'" Autumn had never been skydiving, but she now understood what her grandfather had meant. She sucked in a deep breath of air, as if it could somehow bring the words back to her. She had taken a leap of faith with no idea why, and now all she could hope for was to land on her feet.

All eyes turned to her. She waited for someone to say something, but no one did. Her mind raced. Why had she said it? Her gaze matched Icarus's.

"He could keep driving the kids," Autumn's mom finally said.

"What would he wear?" her father asked.

"He can wear your old tux."

Her parents continued squabbling over the details and Joey began to speak, but Autumn didn't hear any of them. She had fallen into the depths of his eyes as he watched her. She searched for answers. She tried to decipher him, but she was lost.

"I can't," Icarus said. "I'm sorry."

He rose and left.

For a moment, the family all sat in silence. Everything happened so suddenly, Autumn felt as if she were a rollercoaster car that had just jumped the tracks. She rose and followed him out onto the front porch before anyone could stop her. He sat down on the top step, protected from the rain by the awning. She stood in the doorway, waiting for him to acknowledge her.

"Why?" he finally asked. "Why me?"

She wished she knew the answer.

"I don't want to go alone," Autumn said, half-joking, half-serious.

He didn't laugh.

Icarus had always been serious, but he had also always seemed confident.

Now she thought she sensed fear.

Afraid of prom? No, afraid of people! Agoraphobic? Autumn knew that wasn't true either, based on the way he had handled himself at Derek's party.

"Yes," he said.

"Yes, what?"

"Yes, I will go to prom with you," He said it as if he were a child conceding to a bully.

"Icarus," she had meant to tell him that he didn't have to, but instead she answered, "I don't want you to leave."

He turned to her.

"Not yet," she added, trying to sound indecisive.

He rose and walked towards her, stopping when their faces were only inches apart. "I may have been there for you before but you need to know I'm no hero."

"I didn't ask you to be," she replied, growing irritated. "It's just prom, not marriage."

He nodded and went inside the house.

Autumn stood for a moment listening to the rain. Her grandmother had always done that if they had just parked the car, or if they were trying to fall asleep. "Hush," she would say, "listen to the rain." The rain fell heavy.

Autumn wanted him to stay. She wanted to go to prom,

though she hated to admit it, but he seemed so distant...so reluctant. She had hoped that if she did go to the prom with a date and not just her friends, he would show a little enthusiasm about her. Then she remembered her comment, "It's just prom, not marriage," and decided she was overthinking it. He had said yes; she had more time with him to find out his secret. A small part of her couldn't wait to see Derek's face when he saw Icarus again, and she smiled.

She returned to finish dinner with her family. Icarus had already said goodnight and retired. After the family finished their meal, Autumn returned to her bedroom, and after changing into pajamas, began to write. When her alarm clock read nine o'clock, she brushed her teeth and crawled into bed. Her parents came and tucked her in as they did with all of their children, and turned off her light as they left.

Then she lay in bed wide awake. She had asked him to prom and he had said yes. She felt brilliant and stupid, mortified and a bit giddy. She imagined wearing a beautiful prom dress and dancing with Icarus Falls.

When the clock read eleven, Autumn finally got out of bed. She crept over to her desk, and after turning on a night light, flipped through her notebook to the page with the things she had written about him in the margin. She read through them one more time. Then she wrote: *I like him.*

Chapter 25

"You did what?!" Meghan practically screamed. Ian gave a more subtle response of the "I knew it" look. Autumn had been in the building for all of ten minutes, and now felt pretty confident that the whole school knew who would be her date to prom.

"Keep it down," she hissed. "I have to keep him from leaving."

"Because you love him," Ian said.

"No, because I have to solve the mystery of his secret."

"Why is his secret so important?" Meghan asked.

"Well, because..." Autumn began.

"Because you *love* him," Ian repeated.

"Would you cut that out?" Autumn asked, trying to look angry, but trying equally as hard to suppress her laughter. She wasn't stupid enough to believe that she loved him, but she also wasn't dumb enough to deny that she did like him - a lot. Something about the deadpan way Ian said it made her laugh. He would probably be a stand-up comedian someday.

"Alright you two idiots, I'm off to class," she said, leaving them in the hallway and ignoring their parting remarks.

The day passed quickly and smoothly in spite of the many preoccupations on Autumn's mind. It wasn't until she saw Mike waiting by her locker that she realized the day had been saving its misery.

He looked upset, and for a minute, she wondered if someone had bullied him. Then their eyes connected, and she knew that whatever the problem was, it had something to do with her.

"Hey," he said.

"Hey, what's up?"

"Nothing," he answered.

He was either waiting for her to bring it up, or he was trying to muster up the courage to say it himself. Either way, Autumn didn't have the time.

"Well, I'm gonna run. I don't want to be in this place any longer than I have to," she said with a laugh.

He didn't laugh.

"I overheard Meghan talking to some of the girls earlier," he began. "Something about you and Icarus going to the prom."

A small coal of anger began to fan in Autumn. She knew Mike was the jealous type, but she had never expected this.

"Yeah, Icarus is taking me to prom. So what?"

"So, I thought I was."

His voice sounded like the wood of an old coffin while the nails were being pounded into it, thin and ready to break.

Autumn closed her eyes and took a deep breath in frustration before she realized it had been her own fault. She was about to ask him why he was under the impression they were going together, when it hit her: He had asked her to prom and she had wanted to let him off easy, so she had said *I'll think about it.*

Oh poor stupid Mike, she thought. *Strike three.*

This would be the end of the friendship. She could see it in his eyes.

He left without a word.

Chapter 26

The rest of the week, Autumn didn't see Mike, to the point where she began to wonder if he had missed a few days of school. It bothered her that he had taken things so hard, but she figured she would be leaving for college soon anyway. He had probably just taken a day or two off from school and was listening to some breakup music. The thought sickened her on multiple levels.

He will be fine.

She found it ironic how in trying to let him off easy, she had misled him and made it worse.

"What about this one?" Meghan asked as she pulled the hundredth dress off the clearance rack.

Autumn sighed. It was her own fault. She had put off getting the dress. Meghan had known it was going to be a rough time and had offered to join Autumn in her hunt. The racks had been picked clean of anything Autumn's size, style, or interest.

"Too booby," she said.

"You haven't even tried it on," Meghan whined. "Besides who cares?"

Autumn continued sifting the dregs.

"So who are you going with?"

"Not sure. I think maybe Brian."

"You still don't know?"

"I'm tempted to go alone and then dance with all the boys," Meghan said half-serious.

Autumn laughed.

"Do you know if Ian's bringing anyone?" Autumn asked, moving on to a new rack.

"I think he is going with a few of his friends from that movie club he does every Tuesday. How about this?" Meghan asked, pulling another dress from the rack.

Autumn glanced. "Too sparkly."

Meghan checked her watch.

"So how are things with you and Mike?" Meghan asked.

Autumn didn't answer. She never even heard the question. Slowly, she took a red dress from the rack. The soft, gauzy fabric fell perfectly down from the hanger. She ran her hand over the skirt almost reverently and held it up to herself.

"You have to get it," Meghan whispered, in a moment of extreme severity.

"I don't even know if it will fit," Autumn said, checking the tag, knowing that department store sizes were rarely reliable.

"Well go try it on!" Meghan demanded, grabbing her by the hand and ushering her to the fitting room.

Autumn closed the door.

"Please fit," she whispered.

Chapter 27

The day of the prom was an early release so all of the girls could get ready. Autumn knew she couldn't afford to have her nails perfectly manicured and her hair professionally groomed, so as soon as they got home, she locked herself and her mother in her bedroom and the two set to work.

After many hours of toil and stress, Autumn finally felt ready. There was a gentle knock on the door.

"Who is it?" Autumn asked.

"It's dad. Can I come in?"

Autumn nodded to her mother who opened the door slowly.

"How do I look?" Autumn asked.

Her father stood in awe.

"Wow, you look amazing. I want to hug you, but I don't want to ruin anything," he answered.

They all laughed.

"What's up?" Autumn asked.

"You don't have to wear these, but I just thought you might like them."

Her father removed his hands from behind his back, and with them came Autumn's grandmother's long white gloves.

"You can have the pearls on your wedding day, but tonight you can have these if you want them."

Autumn took the gloves and slid them on. They fit perfectly, almost up to her elbow, and though they were old, they were still white as snow. Autumn hadn't wanted to be a princess since she was a very little girl, but as she turned and looked in the mirror again, she felt that she somehow had become one. She looked elegant and regal. The white gloves reminded her of Grace Kelly or Audrey Hepburn.

"I look like a movie star," she said.

Her mother smiled.

"The kids are downstairs waiting," her father said. "Autumn... be safe, but have fun tonight."

Autumn very carefully hugged both of her parents.

"I will."

They exited the room. Autumn's parents descended the stairs first so that everyone could get a good look at her. The whole family had gathered around, and even Father Patrick had come over to see her off.

She took a deep breath and came down the steps.

She saw him, waiting, flowers in hand; Icarus Falls in her father's tux. He looked like a movie star too.

"You look beautiful," he said.

She looked at her feet, feeling her face beginning to turn red. If he really thought she was beautiful, she didn't want her embarrassment to ruin it. As she looked back up her eyes met his, and she knew he hadn't said it out of a sense of necessity. He had meant it.

"Thanks," she answered.

He handed her the flowers, white and red roses. She smelled them and then handed them to her mother to put in a vase. Her mother returned with the corsage and boutonniere which they had left in the refrigerator to keep fresh. Icarus took Autumn's hand and slid the corsage on with ease. She tried to attach the boutonniere to his lapel, but after several attempts, she asked her mother for help, afraid she would stab him or herself.

Her father captured the whole process, taking pictures

with his phone, and once the photos began, they seemed to never stop. They were moved to the stairs, then outside, as family members were switched in and out of each photoshoot to get all of the possible combinations. *'Oh, just one more. No, turn this way. Smile more!'* It amazed Autumn how quickly the experience began to irritate her. She had always wanted to be a famous writer, but she had never thought about the consequences of fame, like Paparazzi.

"Enough!" she commanded, glancing at the clock on her phone. "We have to go."

She hugged her parents goodbye and waved to her siblings as she crossed the lawn with Icarus. All the while her family cheered.

She stepped onto the pavement of the driveway and found the minivan had been removed. Instead, she saw a 2003 Mercury Grand Marquis.

Icarus opened the door on the passenger side like a gentleman, and for a minute, she felt as if she were in an old black and white movie.

"I hope you don't mind taking my car," he said. "It's not much, but it's not a minivan."

She didn't mind at all. Although she had been alone with him while driving many times before, she couldn't help but feel different about it this time.

Autumn noticed his hand hovering over where a shift would be, and wondered if he had driven a stick shift in the past, or if he was leaving his hand available for her.

She hated her excitement. He was going to leave. He knew it and she knew it, but maybe before that happened they could just have one perfect night together.

Chapter 28

They arrived at the Costello, a moderately famous hotel in Manchester ever since Abbot and Costello had performed there back in 1939. Manchester regional high school reserved their function hall every year, much to Autumn's parents' chagrin. Icarus pulled into the parking garage and found a spot at the very top. He put the car in park, and for a moment, they just sat watching the Manchester skyline and the Amoskeag river.

"Thank you," Autumn said breaking the silence.

"For what?"

"For bringing me to prom."

Autumn turned to face him, but his dark eyes never left the lights of the city, even when she slipped off her glove and placed her hand on his. His hand felt warm and rough, both on the inside and out, as if he did a lot of yard work right before heading to a boxing gym. He squeezed her hand gently as they sat in the silence. She had never held hands, not really. She and Mike had when they were children, and she and Ian did on occasion as a sign of support. She had never really just held hands with anyone that she had liked, and though she hated to admit it, part of her wished they would just stay here with the car all night.

"You ready?" he asked.

"What, to go make fools of ourselves?" she asked.

He still just stared into the distance, but she could

see the edge of his smirk.

Oh, Icarus Falls, I think I'm falling for you, she thought and was relieved when it didn't come out of her mouth.

"Wait here," he said and got out of the vehicle.

Autumn watched as he walked around the car and opened her door with a flourish.

"You know my parents aren't here watching," She said, stepping out and taking his extended hand. He looped her arm through his.

"My mother always said, 'Treat a woman like a queen on two days: her prom and her wedding."

"Wow, two whole days," Autumn quipped.

Icarus glared at her as he finished, "and every other day, she is to be treated as a princess."

Normally Autumn would gag, but she saw too much of an opportunity and let it pass.

"You never talk about your mother," she said gently. "Or any of your family for that matter."

"My mother is dead," He commented matter-of-factly, and Autumn felt a hot iron against her heart.

They took the elevator to the ground floor, and were greeted by the chaos of hundreds of excited prom goers as the doors opened into the hotel lobby. Hotel staff came out and ushered everyone into two single-file lines for the security check. It had been implemented more for booze than weapons, and the line moved steadily.

Once they made it through security, Karen, the school photographer and head of the yearbook committee, forced each couple to pose for yet another a picture.

Then they ascended the marble staircase which tapered to a doorway at the top, and entered the function hall.

"Aren't those your friends?" Icarus asked, pointing to Ian and Meghan. As expected, Ian had come with a few of his friends from the school's independent film club and

Meghan had brought her flavor of the week. Autumn waved, and together they walked over. She realized that she had never introduced any of them.

"I can't believe it!" Meghan screamed over the music before adding a girly squeak. "It's finally here."

She gave Autumn a hug.

"And who is this?" she asked very deliberately looking Icarus over.

"Megs, Ian; this is Icarus Falls."

Meghan held out her hand as if she expected him to kiss it. Icarus merely shook it.

"And who is this?" Autumn asked Meghan, whom she could tell had broken into her parent's liquor cabinet before heading over, or rather had probably sat down and had a drink with her parents before they saw her off.

"I'm Sven," Meghan's date said, though he needed no introduction as his father was known around the school for hiring young kids into his company and then cheating them out of proper pay.

Autumn glanced at Meghan who smiled wickedly.

They all took their places at a nearby table, and after visiting the buffet, hit the dance floor. Autumn wasn't one for dancing, but the safety of all of her friends around her helped. The technicolored lights spun around the room and they moved with the music, no one caring how foolish they might look. When the first slow song came on, they all paired off.

Icarus made an oddly formal, polite bow towards her, extending his hand. She found it adorable. Autumn placed her hand in his. He pulled her close and together they swayed gently like two trees in a calm wind.

As the song ended, another with a more upbeat, poppy vibe took its place. Icarus led her by the hand to the edge of the dancefloor, then out through the French doors and onto the terrace. The night was still young, and there were only a handful of others who had decided to take advantage of the same view they had seen from the parking garage.

Icarus brought her to the rail, but this time, instead of watching the city skyline he had eyes only for her.

"Icarus, what happened to you?" Autumn finally asked.

"What do you mean?" he asked.

"I know Icarus isn't your real name. I don't care if your dad is a history teacher nobody names there kid that."

Icarus laughed.

"So why do you *call* yourself Icarus?" Autumn continued. "What happened?"

"I flew too close to the sun," he said without losing any charm, and for the first time, she wondered how many other girls had been hooked by his Icarus Falls smile.

"For once would you give me a straight answer? You're such a drama queen?"

His smile waned. He took her hand and led her to a nearby bench.

"How do you want to remember your prom?"

Autumn stood up, not willing to indulge in more theatrics, but he stopped her with a hand.

"Sit down," he said, motioning to the stone bench.

"When I was 18, I got my girlfriend pregnant on prom night." He confessed, studying her face for a reaction.

"Not all of what I have told you has been a lie," he continued. "My father is a history teacher. He was also a military man. A Catholic military man…"

Autumn began to see why he had taken the name Icarus. He had disobeyed his father. "Catholics don't believe in premarital sex," she stated, familiar with the rule herself.

Icarus looked to the ground. "They also don't believe in abortion…"

Autumn's gut tightened. Though she had never given

much thought to the issue, she realized that for Icarus this had been a life-altering decision; the type of moment that makes you fall from your angel's wings into an ocean of chaos.

Tears had begun rolling slowly down his cheeks, one careening into the other, pushing just a little further until they finally grew too heavy and fell to the ground. He didn't touch them nor did he blink. He simply stared like a dead man at the ground in front of him.

"What did your father say?" Autumn asked, putting her hand over his.

He turned his tear-stained face to hers. "I never told him."

"I don't understand." In spite of all his confessions, Autumn knew he had left something out. Something else remained. Some other sin.

"Icarus...How did you hide it?"

He sighed, "After she told me, we never met at my house. My father never saw her, and I never told him."

Autumn felt as if she had been caught in a riptide. One minute she had been in the shallows, but now she was out further than she cared to admit. He was crucifying himself for something he had done.

"Icarus, you can't punish yourself," she reasoned. "She made her choice."

His eyes met hers and she saw the ferocity of a caged animal.

"Her choice!" he scoffed. "Where the hell was my choice! It wasn't her choice, it was her damn parents! I drove her to the clinic. And there they were with that "we win" look plastered on their damn faces."

His demeanor shifted. As if the rage had suddenly been sapped out of him.

"Then she got out and I - I just started driving..." his words trailed off in a whisper.

Realization dawned on Autumn.

"You left her!"

"I warned her!" he retorted. "I warned her I would leave!"

"You literally just drove away and never looked back?" The words were rushing out of Autumn. His life had begun to fall together like pieces in a puzzle, or perhaps frames in a movie that she seemed to be watching in her mind.

"And face my dad?" he asked. "Hell no! I just got on the highway and drove. I dropped my phone out the window. My name is on the car title so he couldn't report it stolen. When I ran out of money, I swung by local churches and offered to do yardwork for a few dollars to keep me going."

Fury rose up in Autumn.

"You over-dramatic, self-centered idiot!" she roared.

"She killed my kid!" he answered, venom dripping from his words.

"I know! But at any point did you stop to think that maybe she was hurting too? That maybe if her parents really were bearing down on her, that she might need you when the smoke cleared and the dust settled?" The words erupted from her.

Icarus turned towards her, concerned as if he had lit the end of a firecracker and now had second thoughts. Autumn could feel the blood hot in her veins, ready to explode.

"You wouldn't understand," he snapped.

The dim beat from the music inside pulsed, and the crickets could be heard somewhere in the distance. Autumn seethed, reviewing everything in her mind over and over. She felt like someone had pulled the reel on a slot machine in her head, and all of the little dials were spinning around and around. With any luck, they would align and make some sense.

"You have to go back," she said.

She had seen his fear when she had asked him to prom, but now it made sense: prom had been where it had all happened. She saw his look of fear again.

"You have to go back," she repeated.

"I don't *have* to do anything," he stated.

"You're a coward," she said, coldly.

He shot up and for a moment Autumn thought that he would hit her. He didn't.

"You want me to go *back*," he whispered.

Autumn didn't know when she had started crying. Their tears fell in unison.

"I warned you," he growled.

"Just because you admit you didn't study doesn't negate the fact that there will be a test," Autumn said, turning away. She hated the saying. Her mother had said it to her so many times as a child. *I warned you? What, that the truth would hurt?* She didn't care. Whether he was a monster or just a man she didn't care, but she knew now that there would never be a future for her and Icarus Falls. She dried her eyes, imagining all the awful things her mascara would be doing to the rest of her makeup. *Such a silly thought.*

She turned back to face him and she found she was alone.

Chapter 29

I warned you! What fantasy world does he live in? Autumn thought, as she collected herself just enough to make it inside the bathroom and break down. She looked up in the mirror, to see six pairs of eyes staring back. The small group of girls who had gathered within the safety of the bathroom to talk about their dates, took one good look at Autumn and headed straight for the door.

Autumn didn't blame them. She glanced at herself in the mirror, hoping the damage wouldn't be irreversible. Her mascara streaked down her face, but the rest wasn't that bad; she could salvage it if only she could stop crying.

"Are you ok?" a gentle voice asked. Autumn looked up to see a girl standing in the bathroom doorway. They had never spoken before, but Autumn recognized her from Math class. Her name was Charlotte.

Before Autumn could answer, Charlotte left her post at the doorway and gave Autumn a hug. Normally Autumn would have pushed away, but as Charlotte held her, Autumn began to cry again.

When her tears ran dry and her face started to burn, Autumn fought desperately to get control of herself.

"What's wrong?" Charlotte asked, finally releasing Autumn.

"It's nothing," Autumn said. "It's stupid."

"Clearly it's not."

Autumn could tell Charlotte would not take no for an

answer, but if she told her the truth she worried Charlotte might spread it. It was bad enough six or seven girls had seen her crying to begin with. Come Monday, everyone would know that Autumn had cried at prom. The question was, would they know why?

Charlotte looked down at her purse and began rifling for something. Her long blonde hair had been pinned up with loose waves escaping in the back. Her skin shone pale, like an Irish beauty, and when she looked back up, Autumn saw ocean blue eyes.

Maybe she's not a girl from school at all, Autumn thought. *Maybe she's an angel.*

"Let me give you a touch up while you tell me what happened."

Before Autumn could object, Charlotte had already broken out her makeup kit and began making adjustments to Autumn's face.

Autumn knew Charlotte wouldn't tell. She didn't know how, she just knew. However, she feared she wouldn't be able to get through the story before the waterworks began again. She had it under control now. She didn't want to talk about it. She didn't want to think about it.

"He left me," she said, keeping it simple.

Charlotte stopped.

Charlotte had been left before; Autumn could see it in her eyes.

"I'm so sorry."

"Well, tomorrow morning a bunch of our peers will get probably get dumped, so I guess I'm just leading the charge," Autumn said dryly.

Charlotte laughed at this.

"You're Charlotte, right?" Autumn asked. "I don't think we've actually met. I'm Autumn."

Charlotte smiled and began to put away her makeup

kit. "Well, Autumn, you are beautiful as ever."

Autumn turned to the mirror. It was still obvious she had been crying, but Charlotte had done far more than she ever would have been able to.

"Thank you," Autumn said. "You won't tell anyone will you?"

Autumn saw a flash of hurt cross Charlotte's face and wished she hadn't asked. She knew the answer, but she had needed to hear it.

"About what?" Charlotte answered with a wink.

She had clever answers and a witty smile. The girl seemed flawless, and for a moment she reminded Autumn of Icarus.

"Who are you here with?" Autumn asked.

"Derek Mason, do you know him?"

Autumn's heart dropped. *The flawless girl does have a flaw.*

"Yeah," Autumn said, her mind racing. She had to warn Charlotte, but how? *Did you know he's a rapist* seemed a bit too much, but she had to warn this angel.

"I kinda got into some trouble at one of his parties," Autumn admitted.

"Oh?" Charlotte asked.

"Did you see his black eye the other week?"

"You did that?" Charlotte asked in disbelief.

"No," Autumn smiled at the thought. "A friend of mine did. Derek kinda…"

As Autumn searched for the words, a voice from one of the bathroom stalls chimed in.

"He raped her."

Autumn and Charlotte screamed. The stall door directly behind them swung open slowly to reveal Katie, a girl from Autumn's history class.

"Sorry, I didn't mean to scare you." She said, emerging from the stall and crossing to the sink to wash her hands.

"What were you doing?" Autumn demanded.

"Well, I came in to use the bathroom. Then all of a sudden I heard someone come in crying and everybody else leave. I panicked!"

Autumn shook her head in amazement, but then remembered the matter at hand.

"Derek didn't rape me. He *tried* to," Autumn corrected. "Wait, how do you know about that?"

Katie turned off the faucet but didn't turn to dry her hands. Though Katie kept her head down, Autumn could see a small streak in her makeup slowly growing larger in the girls reflection in the mirror.

"Because," Katie said, stifling a sob.

"Oh my God," Charlotte said. "He raped *you*."

Katie took several deep breaths before she continued. "And a few others." She moved for the door grabbing a handful of paper towels on her way. "Look, I just want to enjoy my prom, but you should know he's a scumbag."

Then she opened the door and stepped out into the chaos and revelry.

Autumn looked at Charlotte.

"We should get back out there," Charlotte said, dismissively.

Chapter 30

As Autumn left the bathroom, she stayed towards the back of the hall. Icarus had left. Her friends were somewhere in the crowd, and she didn't feel much like dancing anyway. Her whole high school career had led up to this point, and frankly, it sucked.

She sat down at a table and slipped her cellphone out, beginning to type out a text to her mother explaining how she would be needing a ride home. She hadn't wanted to ride home with her mom in a minivan, but she also hadn't wanted to be left by her date. None of this was what she had wanted. She placed her phone on the table and watched everybody dancing. All of the people with normal lives, and normal dates, and a normal prom. She considered twisting Meghan's arm to give her a ride home, but she knew that would be cruel; Sven had driven.

She watched her peers, grateful for the darkness which shielded her face. She watched as they danced, many of them in a dirty manner, and felt incredibly disenchanted with the whole experience.

She noticed Mike walking over with a drink in his hand.

"Mike! What are you doing here?" Autumn asked.

"It's my senior prom. I'm allowed to be here, aren't I?" Mike answered, looking around as if he had somehow stepped on a landmine.

"Yes, I just figured," Autumn began. "I mean, I haven't

seen you. Who are you here with?"

"Myself," Mike said, proudly.

Autumn felt like a jerk for asking.

"Look, Mike –"

He held up a hand to silence her.

"Bygones be bygones, done is done," he said, quoting *the Iliad*. "We can't all be blessed with good looks and that 'man of mystery' aura."

A sense of guilt grew in Autumn with each of Mike's words, and Autumn knew she deserved it.

"Where is the old chap anyway?" he asked, slipping into more of a Gatsby role as he waved his glass of non-alcoholic punch.

"Actually, he left."

Mike laughed disingenuously, studying her face. He realized she was telling the truth.

"Autumn, are you ok?" he asked.

"Not really," she said with a forced laugh, involuntary tears slipping out of the corners of her eyes.

Mike produced a handkerchief from his pocket and reached for her.

"Don't you dare!" she commanded, starting to laugh through her tears. "You're so sweet, it's gross! Give me that! I can wipe my own face."

He handed her the handkerchief and she dried her eyes with a smile.

"What happened?" he asked, sitting down at the table.

Autumn still didn't want to talk about it, but Mike had been so gracious he deserved to know. He waited quietly listening through the whole story, and when it came to an end he didn't make a show of it. He gave no lecture or teaching moment, no questions if Icarus would be back.

"Do you want to go home?" he asked.

"No," she said. "No, I think I would like to dance. This

isn't how I want to remember my senior prom."

"I think your friends are over on the left towards the front," Mike said.

"I can't see them," she said. "Would you escort me?"

He nodded and stood up, motioning for her to follow. As they entered the crowd, Autumn took his hand and once they got to her friends, she didn't let go of him. Mike was not much of a dancer, and she knew he hated being out on a dance floor. She also knew that if she made him, he would stay, and as selfish as it might be, this was how she wanted to remember the end of high school; in a beautiful dress, dancing, with her friends.

When the night ended, Mike offered to give Autumn a ride back to her house. He had her wait at the door while he brought the car around.

As Autumn stood waiting and reflecting on the night's events, Charlotte caught her eye, riding by in her father's truck, and winked at her. Derek stood on the sidewalk, disgruntled and alone.

Chapter 31

At the end of the summer, Autumn left for college. She attended Ave Maria University in Florida, which she deemed far enough away from her family. By the end of her four years and after some additional traveling, she found herself wanting more and more to return to New Hampshire. After graduating, she moved back in with her parents while she looked for a job.

A week after Autumn returned, Mike came calling, and after a bit of persuasion, the two began dating in a serious way.

Autumn often wondered about the stranger they had let into their lives, and though she never saw him again, she did receive a letter shortly after she and Mike had begun dating. It had been four years since that summer.

It read:

Dear Autumn,

I hope you and the family are doing well. I apologize for not writing sooner, but as I am sure you understand, this is not an easy letter to write. I have often woken in the night thinking of you and those illusion shattering words you said to me. "You coward. You have to go back." After I left you at the prom (I'm sorry – I never should have done that and honestly I should send you a whole second letter simply apologizing for it), I drove most of the night. I headed south until I hit the

Carolinas. I was angry. I had known the truth, and frankly the truth had been too hard to bear, so I made my own truth... and then you came along and screwed it up. As I drove away that night, I told myself that I was simply in love. In love with love. You and Jessica had been collateral damage. But your words stuck with me like the ghost of Christmas Future, quiet and terrifying.

I had stopped for two days to rest and to write. Then when I got back in the car, I found myself heading back, heading home.

My father was overjoyed to see me.

Then I went to see Jessica. I will say her parents were not thrilled to see me, but that's a story for another time.

She opened the door with a baby in her arms.

I have often thought about it all...that summer out in New Hampshire and all of the lies I had let myself believe, and in the past few years I have come to a realization. I was not in love with love. I don't believe that's possible. I was in love with romance. You see, a gunfight in a movie might be romantic, or a whirlwind relationship. Romance is easy. It's the beginning of the journey when everything is fresh and exciting, but love...love is hard. Love is saying you are sorry for screwing up and genuinely trying to be better. Love is waking up to the sound of a screaming baby. Love is waking up next to the same person over and over...we must be honest if we are to love.

I missed the first year of my child's life, and if it hadn't been for you and your honesty, I might have missed the whole thing. I cannot thank you enough.

Sincerely,

Icarus Falls

About the Author

Eric Tamburino is the American author of *Where Man And Monster Meet: A New Collection of Fairy Tales* and this YA coming of age novel, *Icarus Falls*. He graduated from college with a bachelor's degree in communications and works as an instructional video designer/customer success specialist.

In early school years, he struggled, particularly with reading and writing, but always found it easier to learn when information was presented in story form.

He began his writing journey in high school when he started writing short stories more for the therapeutic aspect of the craft rather than the intention of writing a book. After college, he rewrote each story which turned into the fairy tale anthology: *Where Man And Monster Meet.*

A comic book lover and movie fanatic, Eric currently lives in New Hampshire with his wife and has several more books planned.

Contact: wheremanandmonstermeet@gmail.com
https://wheremanandmonstermeet.com

Acknowledgments

I would like to say thank you to a great many people who assisted me in the completion in this book, some of whom include: Loretta C., Luke S., Chris L., Brittany M, Tara D, my wife, and of course my father. There are too many more to list here but please know that I am grateful.